I Fell For A Street Menace

By: Nakeria Hendley

Copyright 2017

Other Titles By Nakeria Hendley:

His Gutta Chic 1-3

There Are No Rules To Love: Ke'maine and Rajah 1-3

Love Won't Let Me Leave

I Fell For A Street Menace 1-2

Contact Me!

Facebook: Author Nakeria Hendley

Reading Group: Author Nakeria Hendley

Chapter 1

Travis

"Aye bro, hand me the remote."
"Nigga, get it ya damn self. I ain't ya maid."
I sucked my teeth and got up to get the remote. This nigga was always on some bullshit, but if he asked you to do something, he expects you to do it. That's the shit I don't like, and half the time why we bump heads. Akeem was the oldest sibling. My mom had four boys, and I was the second in line. I kicked his feet off the table and sat back down. He sneered at me, but I wasn't worried about him. It wouldn't be the first time we were about to come to blows, and damn sure not the last.

Dig this, I'm Travis, and the most chill brother of us all. We all share the same mom but have different dads. I'm the only one whose dad is in my life and has been since a lil nigga was a baby. I guess that has a lot to do with my demeanor and the way I carry myself. I have a job down at the airport, no kids, and a lil shawty who I live with, but I spend most of my time right here at my momma's crib.

This will always be home. Emana doesn't like how much of a momma's boy I am, but she ain't went nowhere either.

"Yo! Why y'all in here when it's popping outside, my nigga?" Hasan came in all hype with our youngest brother, Jequell, right behind him.

I took a good look at both those niggas and knew they were high as shit. I smoke too, but I ain't have shit on those two chimneys'.

"What's going on outside that ain't always going on outside, homie?" Akeem spoke up in his always too calm voice.

This nigga barely ever raises his voice, and when he does, you better run for the hills. 95% of the time he is collected. Even if he is mad, he would still come off calm until he just throws them hands.

Niggas around here respected us, and most feared us. When it came down to it, we were nothing to play with. But, it's always a chum ass nigga who wants to try his luck, and every time they do, an example is made out of them.

"Here this nigga go," Jequell mumbled.

Since it wasn't shit on TV and it was nice out, I stepped out on the porch with them to see what the hype was about. The block was definitely hitting for something today. I pulled up a chair and tilted my cup of lean. Yeah, I did the dirty Sprite thing. It made niggas sleepy, but it mellowed me out.

A group of young girls walked past switching extra hard and waving at us. I shook my head, but Jequell and Hasan entertained them hot pussy cakes. I was every bit of 26, and messing with girls under 22 was a turn off to me. They were immature, ain't have shit to offer, and wanted to party all the time. Emana was the complete opposite. She was actually 28, the same age as Akeem, and carried herself with class.

That's why sometimes I think she's too good for me. I fuck up a lot and can't help it, but she stays even after she threatens to leave. She works at a bank downtown making nice bread, but her family has money. I fucked with her most because she wasn't the type to sit on her ass and spend their money up. She didn't act stuck up or talk down on people.

When I saw her at the Gucci Mane concert with a few of her friends, she stood out the most, and I knew before I left that night that I would get her number.

Chapter 2

Hasan

"Hey Hasan."
I stopped brushing my hair and looked at the lil skeeze.
I smiled, showing my gap, and gave her a head nod. I
knew what she wanted, and I ain't mind dropping it off
in her draws either. I got up and walked over to her.
She looked a lil young, but I didn't discriminate. As
long as you were over 18, I was boning, on the hood.
"What it do, young," I said upon reaching her.
"What y'all finna do?"
"Shit, 'bout to smoke and sip."
"Oh yeah, can we chill with y'all?"
That was basically the offer right there. I told her let's
roll then. My momma was gon' be there at any minute,
and if she pulled up and saw a bunch of lil bitches on
her porch, we were all getting cussed out. I had a lil
spot around the corner just for the hoes, though. Quell
was busy talking to her friend, but I gave him that
gesture, so he'd know what time it was. I let bro know
what was popping off and asked did he want parts, but
he frowned like I had offended him.
I forgot his lil bullshit policy about females. Pussy is
pussy, though. Fuck all that goofy age bullshit.
Speaking of which, "Aye where ya ID at?"
She gave me a confused look as if she didn't know
what I was talking about.
"You don't have an ID?"

Looking nervous, she shook her head no. That did it, her lil young ass wasn't even 18. Tryna get a nigga cased up. I should shoot her lil ass for fucking with my emotions and shit.

"Fuck on somewhere, crim." I gritted mad as shit that she had fucked my nut up.

Travis started laughing at me, and Keem was standing in the door shaking his head.

"Ha ha these nuts right in ya mouth."

"You seem upset, bro."

I shot his ass the bird. He knew damn well that had me hot. It seems like all these lil bitches around be trying me. They don't do that shit with them niggas. I slipped up one time, so now I check IDs from here on out. I was fucking this one shawty, and she was a freaky lil bitch too. She even had a nigga catching small feelings, but one day she did some nut shit and I let it slide. When she kept doing it, I had to do a background check. Come to find out, she wasn't 20. She was 17 and had a birthday coming up when she would have been 18.

I threw her ass away like a piece of trash. I don't do liars, bruh. At the time, I was just 22 and was hitting everything. She was the only one who had me doing extra shit. I felt like a sucka when I found out her real identity. I still see her every now and then, but I look right past her ass like she ain't there. I know it be killing her 'cause she always has this long look on her face like she wants to say something but knows better.

A nigga ain't never have a problem embarrassing nobody. You do some crafty shit, and it's either catch these hands, get put on blast and still catch these hands, or I shoot ya ass, point blank. She's a female, so I screened her shit in front of the whole way. She ran off crying, but I didn't feel an ounce of sympathy for her ass.

Don't play me, and I won't play you. It's that simple. Anyway, I'm Hasan, the craziest one of the bunch. I jumped off the porch real early, and now I can't seem to stop. But don't get it fucked up, I don't want to stop. As I get older, I get more reckless and turn savage over any small thing. My mom tells me all the time that I better slow down, or she gon' be planning my funeral. I tell her right back where the money is for it too. As long as I bleed the same as any other nigga, I will never chill.

Taking a couple pulls from Travis' loud, I went back to brushing my hair. I had super stupid waves that I had a tendency to brush all day every day when I wasn't doing anything. Since my mom said she wasn't sure who my pop was, it was between two niggas. I'on know the guy, but I can say he blessed me with a good head of hair. The ladies go crazy when they see my shit spinning like a Ferris wheel.

All of us are dark except Travis' bitch ass. He the only bright nigga that you can see in the dark. The rest of us have that smooth, milk chocolate skin. Guess we took after our momma. She's dark skinned too with the same kind of skin. We all were over 6 feet too, with me being the tallest at 6'5". I get asked all the time how tall I am, and if they are cute, I tell them my dick is just as long.

A filter? Naw, I didn't know what that was. I speak my mind, and I spit real authentic shit. Either you can take me, or you can't. And when you can't, just stay the fuck from around me. I get nervous when a mafucka ain't acting normal. And if I'm nervous, ain't shit finna be pretty.

Chapter 3

Akeem

It was time for me to raise up. I had stuck around to see my mom, but she was taking too long to get there. I had shit to do. These niggas looked like they were gonna sit there all day. That was cool, for them, anyway. I had some people who owed me money, and today was the last day that I let anything slide. I like to give a mafucka the benefit of the doubt. Give you a chance to handle ya shit the correct way. But when I feel like you ducking me and ignoring me, then I have to boss the fuck up on you.

I was a quiet nigga, only spoke when necessary. If I have to get out of character then you know what time it is. When I'm riled up, it ain't no coming down until I'm ready. I send my own self into a major headache. That's why I like to chill. My brain is so menacing that I think of all kind of ways to kill me a nigga. I will walk around with a bible that has the inside cut out and my gun laying right there.

Niggas never know how I'm coming, and I'm a keep it like that. So, today, I may have to shed some blood if that money looking funny.

"Yo, crim, what you 'bout to get into? I can see it in ya eyes, and you know I want in, nigga," Hasan said, watching me think.

I looked at him and smirked. That was one nigga who will always be on go, no matter what. Rarely have I gone with anybody to do my dirt; if it's no witnesses, then it's no snitches. But, on occasion, Hasan has accompanied me.

"Be ready in an hour. Meet me at my spot, I'm gone," I told them and walked down the steps.

"I thought you said you were waiting on Mommy."

"I was, but I ain't got all day either," I said over my shoulder.

My car was parked up the street, but I walked right past it and footed it to my crib. We all had our own spots except Quell. He had the bread to move, but he loved staying with our mom. I think she loved that shit too as much as she runs her mouth and talks shit. All she ever did when we were growing up was say, "I can't wait 'til y'all get old enough to get out my damn house." That shit became a broken record over the years.

I moved out way before my time, even had her put her name on my lease for me. I liked to have my space, and living with my ma wasn't allowing me have that. I made it to the crib and took a quick shower before changing into all black. Threw a skully on and checked my guns. I had a favorite one, and that was my .45. That lil big bitch was pretty, and did some pretty art when painting niggas.

I heard stern tapping at my door, so I picked up my phone and switched to the cameras. When I saw that it was Hasan, I hit a few buttons, and the locks turned for him to enter. I had the best high-tech security system around, and my brothers had the same. Our life was nothing to be played with, and we treated it as such. My spot was in the cut, but I wasn't hiding either.

"Yo, bruh, you ready?" Hasan asked all amped up. I shook my head, grabbed the rest of my shit, and exited the crib. Hitting them same buttons to lock up.

Chapter 4

Jequell

I laughed so hard my damn stomach started hurting. My mom had pulled up cussing the moment her car door opened and she stepped foot on the pavement. The shit was comical to me; I never took her serious when she got to going off. Half the time it be about nothing. I was convinced that she just likes to hear herself talk.

"Keep thinking it's funny, Jequell, and I'm a take this broom right up side ya fucking head. You watch," she threatened. I backed out of her reach and kept right on laughing. Travis ended up joining in too. She was mad and was trying to put us both out. I waved her off and took a seat on the couch, using one foot to take my shoe off. Since them young bitches had fucked up the whole spot earlier, I was gon' chill 'til my lil bitch got off.

By the way, I'm Jequell, the baby of my bros. There are some perks that come with being the youngest. These niggas were ruthless as hell growing up, but I never backed down from any of them. Cold gat! While Hasan was the savage of us, I was the gutta brother. I used to want to be like his ass so bad, just watching all the crazy shit he would do. But then I caught my own wave and ran with it. These niggas know. I had to give it up a couple times for them to understand to play with their bitch and not us.

"Where is Hasan and Akeem? He said he would be here when I got home"

"He was here, but you was taking too long. You already know that nigga ain't got no time to just sit around and wait on nobody," I told her as I looked down at the pic that had just came through my phone of this lil slut bitch who want the dick bad.

As bad as I wanna fuck her, I haven't, and that's saying a lot for a nigga like me. These bitches loved street savages.

That's why I haven't committed myself to a full-blown relationship. I wasn't ready period! I fucked with my lil baby 'cause she was loyal, but even she knew what was up. I was only 22, and being locked down wasn't my twist. I kicked it with Moms and Travis 'til around 9:30. Since I planned to lay up for the night, I decided to surprise Shyanne and be outside her job before she clocked out.

I know I be confusing what we have by doing lil sweet shit that a man supposed to do for his girl, but that was just me. I had a soft spot for her, I just didn't want to hurt her. With 10 minutes to spare I pulled in the parking lot of her job and cut the lights. She worked at this clothing store that all the thot bitches go to shop. I hated her job because every day she came home with a story about what some other bitch said.

That also was another reason we haven't tied this shit up. She always had the gossip in what we got. I don't be wanting to hear that shit, and most the time it be lying ass bitches who wish they were on the team. If we fucked, it was just that, a fuck. Only bitch that got the dick more than once was Shyanne.

She and her boss walked out after locking up the store. When she about to walk with her to her car, I hit the lights on.

She put her hand up to shield her face, and I laughed because I knew she about to snap. Opening my door, I got out and stood next to it.

"Jequell, I swear you are such an asshole, but I love ya dumb ass," she fussed

"Hey, Jequell. Bye y'all," her boss said while getting in her car.

I gave her the head nod and got back in my car, ready to pull off.

"Baby, what you doing here? I thought you were going to be busy."

"Change of plans, Shy," I said and handed her a bag of her favorite food. Barbecue chicken with mac and cheese, and collard greens from Cecily's.

She smelled it and closed her eyes. I shook my head at her antics. This girl was crazy about that platter. She reached over and squeezed my dick while planting her juicy ass lips on mine. Damn girl tried to suck my damn lips off my face.

"I love you so much, man. What would I do without you, Jequell?" she asked in a sing song voice.

I just laughed at her. She was so dramatic with everything she did. I think that is what draws me to her. It was rarely any boring or dull moments with her. We went to her crib, and I kicked my shoes off again at the door. It was something about being in some fresh socks that had me wanting to take my shoes off all the damn time. Shiid, even when a nigga was driving I slid them off. Weird, huh? Well, I don't give a fuck anyhow.

"Come on, babe"

I turned around to Shyanne standing there naked, hands on her hips, with a smirk on her face. I tripped over the carpet getting to her. This was the shit I could get used to. Shy ran us some bath water. When she got in from work, she always wanted to take a shower or bath with me. I don't know why it was mandatory, but I never asked. Even if I had just got out the shower before coming there, she would make me get my black ass back in.

Crazy part is, after being out in the streets all day and coming there, these lil moments with her be what a nigga needed. A street nigga can front like having a down ass bitch wasn't a necessity after a long ass day all he wanted. But I'm here to tell you that this shit here, nigga. This right here was love. I couldn't help but place kisses along her shoulder blade.

"Hmmm, babe, you better stop if you not ready to go rounds with me."

I forgot to mention that her ass was a beast. I could never just get a quick nut off and chill. She had to go 'til SHE tapped out. Half the time, my balls be sore from fucking around with her, then other times I treat her ass so good she goes to sleep sucking on her pinky. And she doesn't even suck her fingers on the regular. Tonight, I was ready, though, so I kept right on teasing her lil ass. Her head dropped back, and if I hadn't moved mine out the way, she would have busted my damn nose with that heavy mafucka. I was ready to get this show popping, so I stopped and grabbed the sponge, soaking her body up. I liked to see the suds trail down her body. That shit did something to me for some reason. Shy cocked her legs wide for me, so I threw the sponge and went face first. Her pretty pussy was nice and waxed.

Being the pro that I am, I sucked on her shit under water. I felt her leg getting ready to shake a little. She used to be so embarrassed that her legs would shake bad from the way I ate her out. Now, she loved it and expected it to happen every time.

"Rrrrgh, damn it, Quell!" she growled.

If I ain't know no better, I would have thought a fucking dog was in this bitch. I made her soul cry with this lethal tongue. Only her and one other girl can say they got this kind of treatment from me. And the only reason why the other bitch got it was because I was gone off that molly. I had to stop taking them bitches. I was not myself, and did a bunch of dumb shit on them. Even Shy cut me off for a while. I acted like I ain't give a fuck, but I was missing the shit out of her ass.

One day, I just showed up at her apartment, yoked her up on the wall, and rearranged her insides with long dick! She got to singing the tune I wanted to hear, and shit been cool ever since. She made me promise to never pop them again, and I agreed.

Chapter 5

Hasan

We hopped off our bikes and parked them under a tree. I sparked as Keem leaned against the tree stroking his beard. I already knew what that meant, he was in deep thought about how he wanted to play this shit out if it didn't go as planned. I was cool either way. If it was a light situation then that's what it was. But if it was one where it called for us to do a nigga dumb dirty, then I was with that too. I will always and forever be with the shits!

My ass started to hurt sitting on that ground. I hadn't asked him who we were waiting for and where they were. This nigga will sit there all night if he had to. The few times I went with him, I had to learn to be patient. I was so on go all the time that I will get ya ass in broad day. Fuck waiting and preying. If it was an opportunity to get at ya ass, then I was gon' seize the moment. He tapped me then got up and started toward two niggas coming out of this crib. I hopped up and jogged over to him.

"Aye, Van. Damn, what's up, my nigga?" Keem said ever so calmly.

The nigga Van looked like he saw his soul leave his body.

"Uh, Akeem. Man, what's good bro," he stuttered, barely getting it out.

The nigga he was with was in defense mode. I'd never seen him before, so I figured he ain't know who the hell we were.

"Let me get this straight. I look out for you, and in return, you were supposed to have my bread on deck immediately, right?" Bro folded his arms across his chest, squinting his eyes at Van's bitch ass.

"I need more time, bro. Shit ain't work out like I had planned. Nigga took a few more losses along the way. You know how that shit go."

"Nah, you completely right, I do know how that shit go. But I missed the part where you were supposed to reach out to me and let me know what's up. See, you failed to do that, and on top of that, you been treating me like I'm ya bitch. Play with her, though, my nigga, not my fucking money," he said with venom dripping from his voice.

The nigga standing next to him finally spoke up. I knew it was eating at him from the facial expressions he gave. I just let him dig his own grave, though.

"Hol' up. Van, why is you sitting up here explaining yaself? If you don't have it then you don't have it!" Akeem whistled, and chuckled along with it. Van looked at his mans with the biggest eyes I have ever seen. Guess he knew what was about to happen. Keem hit this nigga with one of the hardest right hooks. I'm sure that shit could be heard for miles. I knew that nigga's jaw was broken on first hit.

He then pulled out a knife, and with one swift motioned, jabbed it at least 70 times into Van. He was gurgling blood up like mouth wash. I jumped up and down, hype. This type shit excited me, and I had a fetish for seeing blood leaking from a fuck nigga! I lifted my pump and blew dude's face off. Bro took his baby out and splattered Van's head like a watermelon. We coolly walked back over to our bikes and pedaled off into the night. That was super easy. I sometimes like when a nigga would give us a run for our money. That barely happened because of the name we made for ourselves, though. I rode my bike back to my crib and Bro did the same. We didn't stay that far apart from each other. When I got in, I checked to make sure he was good, and he was.

At times like this, I wished I had a buss it baby to come home to. The single life does get tiring after a while. I mean, you have pussy at ya beck and call, but even that gets old. I don't trust nobody, so I could never get completely comfortable around any chick I deal with. And they be trying too hard to be my bottom bitch. Shit could never just flow. After getting cleaned up, I lay across my couch with just my boxers on and my eyes closed.

Sometimes I needed just peace and quiet to collect my thoughts. I do so much in the streets that a nigga don't know if he's coming or going. I was drifting off when I heard a tapping noise. It was only me there, so any sound was suspect to me. I flicked the cameras on TV. Checking the perimeter of my spot. I ain't see shit, but that didn't stop me from getting up and checking it out.

With my gun aimed at anything moving, I still didn't see anything. A damn raccoon jumped out of my trash can, and I blew his damn top off. I had been meaning to kill that bastard anyway. His ass was tearing my trash up, and I hated picking up trash. Satisfied that I had finally got that fucker, I curled back up on the sofa with one hand in my boxers. It was a lil nippy in there. My alarm went off around 4:30 in the morning. It was time to get up and go shake shit down. I hustled here and there, but that wasn't my twist. I liked to take your shit, especially if you were getting a major dollar. I tried selling my own weight, but I be fucking that money up. I'd just rather rob you of yours.

I brushed my teeth and washed my face then I went into the room where I have clothes just for gritty shit. I found some black sweats, the hoodie to match, and some all black Forces for my feet. I even had special gloves that I wear too. Ready to go, I hopped in my jinther, which was a junky wheel for situations such as this, and cruised to the other side of town.

The streets were quiet, and niggas were still asleep. Can't call yaself a hustla if you ain't out at the crack of dawn getting that dollar, right? I parked my whip behind this big ass dumpster that stank. Holding my hand up to my nose, I climbed the back steps to this crib I had been eyeing for months. I'm not a petty stick up boy; I sit on you for months to see what kind of chicken you bringing it. If I don't feel like it's worth me even trying, then consider yaself lucky.

I don't go around just snatching shit. I make sure whatever I get lasts me for some time. This nigga, Lucci, had been banking in that dough. They close down shop around 2:30. All his workers dip, and almost every time, it's just him there by himself for a few hours, and then he leaves. It was now 5:20, and any minute he was gon' hit the door. I tightened my gloves and checked my chamber on my guns. Honestly, I didn't think I needed my straps, but I go nowhere without them. His shooters had gone home already; big mistake on his part. Few niggas respected him, so they never thought about snuffing his ass. I ain't give a rat's ass about him. He had something I wanted, and this morning, after 3 months, I was gon' get it.

The door finally opened, and walking out was him and another dude. I should have been surprised that someone else was with him today, but it didn't make a difference. If any of them hoe niggas wanted to play super heroes, then I was gon' open their chest. I slid from behind the wall and stood in the open.

"Hey guys, good morning," I said to fuck with them. I knew there was going to be a tough acting one. It always is.

"Fuck you want, nigga?" the taller one said as he clutched.

See, in this game, you can't just pull or draw ya hammer and not use it. He was so busy trying to protect his manhood and show that he 'bout it, that he lost his life that quick.

Pow!

One single shot to his forehead and he tumbled down the steps. Lucci's fat ass was sweating, and it was a lil' chilly out this morning.

"Now, where were we? Oh, yeah, so what's in the bag?"

He pulled it tighter, but just stared at me. He never said a word. Not that I cared, but I didn't plan to be out here all morning with his ass either. I raised my gun and popped him in both knees. His bones popped out and he hollered to high heavens. Since both his hands were trying to cover his knees, I took the bag and walked off.

That nigga was screaming he gon' kill me and whoop, whoop. I wasn't worried about all that. My face was covered, and so was every part of my body except my eyes. Just to throw niggas off, when I sweep down on them, I use green colored contacts. They will never know it's me.

I drove the jinther back over to my side and parked. With the bag in hand, I went back in the crib, stripped down, and got to counting the profit. Ooh wee! I made out with 478 grand.

Yeah, that nigga definitely bloody. He just took a loss for half a milli. Oh well, I was still a lil' tired, so I ate a big ass bowl of cereal and climbed in my bed. Turned my phone on DO NOT DISTURB and took my ass back to sleep!

Chapter 6

Travis

Emana was dragging me down to this event at the park. I told her ass I didn't want to go, but she bitched all night and day about it. I didn't want my pussy to get revoked from a nigga, so here the fuck I am. A few people were there who I knew and folk from her job. I had my phone out watching porn while she spoke to everybody.

I never understood these types of events. And because I wasn't a real people person, I tried to avoid them at all cost.

Mana lived for this shit; the attention, and even the hate. My baby was on the border of thick and BBW, but I loved every bit of that shit. Ain't a skinny bitch out there fucking with her, on the hood. She was fairly tall, 5'9" so she carried her weight well.

Jequell hit me up asking where I was. He was relieved to know I was there. His lil momma, Shyanne, was bringing his ass along too. I thought I was mad, but this lil nigga was cussing so bad he wasn't even making sense anymore.

I stood off and put my phone away as I watched my baby interact with these clowns. A few niggas were getting wet at the mouth, but that shit didn't bother me. I knew just as well as she did that all that was me. I wasn't no insecure ass nigga, even though I knew I could do better with a lot of shit when it pertains to our relationship. She winked at me just as Quell walked up with his face all broke.

"Nigga, fix ya face. Shit, you here now."

"Fuck out of here, crim. Shy weirdo ass cussed me out so bad she couldn't breathe for a second. Shit scared the piss out of me. I had to run to the bathroom dragging her with me, so she wouldn't die while I drained the main vein."

I fell out laughing at this clown. He was dead serious too.

"And I guess that made you guilty enough to come?" He looked at me with an annoyed expression, and I started laughing again. The dysfunctional shit they had going on was beyond me. Bro and I chilled while the ladies did their thing. Glad his ass did show up because I would have been dried out. He kept me laughing and entertained.

"Aye, you remember that mark ass nigga I was telling y'all about?"

I looked at him and shook my head. He gave me the head nod toward the nigga he had spoke on.

"We can go out to the lot and see what's up, but doing anything right here would be suicidal, bro." I had to plant that in his head. Jequell and Hasan are quick to do some dumb shit without thinking.

He led the way out to the lot. Even though I didn't have beef, I mean that I knew of in these streets, I stayed strapped up, shawty. We waited leaned against a car for the ol' faggot nigga.

"The man of the hour," I said, spotting him first coming from the opposite direction and looking back. Quell took off toward him. Without warning, he started beating that nigga's ass. He did try to fight back, but bro dicked that fool, on the hood. I caught him as he pulled out his tulie and pushed him away. People started coming out to the lot, and it was almost a homicide. Both our phones started to go off.

Jequell walked away madder than he was when he arrived. I shook my head and went the other way as I answered Mana . I took her to the crib and got her straight before I left back out to go check on my lil brother.

Hasan and Jequell were both on the porch blowing when I got there. I slapped hands with Has, and turned to Quell to see if he was smooth. It appeared that way to the normal eye, but I knew this nigga, and steam was coming out his ears.

We heard tires screeching to a halt in front the crib and immediately went for our hittas. Out hopped Shy's crazy ass. We all sucked our teeth because this girl can really clown.

"Oh, so this is where you ran off to after I called ya phone a million times, niggahh!"

I hated the way she pronounced nigga, that shit got under my skin. She climbed the steps, popping off and punching her hand and shit. Typical black girl antics.

"Jequell Dareese Blitz!"

Oh shit, she done called this nigga's whole government out. Both me and Has fell out tipping.

"Aye, Shyanne, do me a favor and gone home. I'm not in the mood to deal with this shit right now, crim. I'll buss ya head," he told her, shutting her parade down.

"Oop! Well, what the fuck is wrong with you?"

Jequell got up, swooped her ass, and took her back to her car. She had his shirt in a death grip and wouldn't let go. Next thing we knew, Shy hauled off and smacked bro's expression from pissed to blazing. I had to jump in or else he would have killed her then cried about it later.

Once I was able to get them separated, she got back in her car, and left the same way she came, screeching.

"Watch I beat her ass later, bro. Always on that extra shit. She sees I'm not in a playing mood, yet she still gotta fuck with a nigga." He went clean the fuck off. All we could do is listen to him vent. Has bitch ass ain't even attempt to help me. He just sat there shaking his head. I chopped it up with my momma for a minute as she made me and Emana plates to go.

Akeem walked through the door with his shoulders up and back wide. He be lifting them weights on the regular. Now, I ain't no small nigga. 6'3" light skinned nigga, 230. I'm a solid nigga, but this fool was husky.

"Look at this nigga looking like he fresh out the slammer," Has clowned on him.

Akeem ain't pay him the least bit of attention. He was used to us firing shots. Walking right past us, he went into the kitchen.

"Bro, you can't have ya bitch pulling up and acting out on you like that. Other mafuckas see that and lose respect for you, then how you gon act?" Has tried to school Jequell.

I had to agree with him on that too. If niggas see ya bitch getting away with disrespecting you, then later, they gon' feel liable to do that shit too.

"Nigga, ain't none of these mafuckas stupid enough to try me, and if they do, I ain't never been a hoe nigga!"

"Aye, man, I'm just saying, get her wild ass in check. That's all."

"I got this shit over here, Hasan. Worry about ya lonely ass dick."

The look on Has' face was the bid. His ass wasn't expecting to get that thrown out there.

"Both of y'all shut the hell up! All that damn hollering in my shit. Y'all wanna come at each other's neck, take that shit outside. But tell Shyanne ass, she gon' have to see me. Pull up at my house again with the fuckery!"

And Momma has spoken.

Quell stood up and left. He was big mad that everybody was on his case. We were only looking out for him. He was the youngest and didn't know it all yet. Grown man or not.

Chapter 7

Akeem

I was in the kitchen stuffing my face and listening to Has tell Jequell to get his bitch together. I ain't have a clue as to what those niggas were talking about until my mom told me that Shy had pulled up cutting up. I just shook my head. I wish my girl would act a whole bitch in public. She had better beat me to the crib and be gone by the time I get there. I don't tolerate clown shit period. The smallest thing could have me pissed.

I had just got off work and went to the gym. I liked to keep my appearance up and muscles flexing. Since I was the shortest at 6'0", I was the huskiest. Nigga had power packed behind any punch I threw. I try to avoid having to put my hands on niggas because my shit is lethal, but it doesn't always work out that way.

I cleaned my dish that I ate out of and went back out to the living room. Since Jequell was all in his feelings, I would talk to him later. I had been hearing some shit going on, and though I wasn't sure what it was, I wanted to check into it. I had to get my brothers on board.

"Yo, lets rap."

I went out front first and took a seat. The other two came out behind me. Once they got situated, they looked at me, wondering what I was about to say.

"Listen, it's some females who been setting niggas up and taking them for everything they have. Some they leave alive and some they off. I wanna find out who the fuck these bitches are and what's the game plan, ya dig me? Where they from? And why they here?"

"Oh, hell nawl. You know what any of them look like?" Has asked, scooting to the edge of his seat.

"That's the problem, I don't know what they face look like, but I know they supposed to be some pretty bitches. This shit was brought to my attention, and I can't do this shit on my own. I'll run it down to Quell. I mean, if any of y'all see him first then handle that." I got up to dip, leaving them with their thoughts.

I wasn't sure what was to come with these bitches, but something ain't sitting right with me, and when that feeling comes about, I got to jump on it.

I slid on this lil momma that I buss down from time to time. She was cool folk, but I couldn't personally wife her. She may be cool, but she lies for no apparent reason, and that shit turns me all the way off. That's why I said time to time. Real definition of 'something to do when there is nothing to do,' and I been down the road of trying to make shit work with her. My heart just won't love the way she wants it to.

"What's up, Lyn?" I greeted when I walked through her front door.

Her backside was one for the books, and it was all natural. My brothers liked girls with a lil weight on them, but I was the total opposite. Ralyn stood 5'4" and wasn't bigger than 168. I picked her ass up all the time like light weight.

With a smile graced upon her face, she turned around with her arms out for a hug.

"Hey, Akeem. I missed you, baby."

"Well, I'm here," I responded.

I couldn't show emotion even if I tried. I just wasn't that nigga. You only had to steer me wrong once, and I'll deal with you accordingly. Lyn didn't personally do anything life threatening, but the bullshit that comes out her mouth painted a different picture of her to me. So, when I'm passing time, I'll shoot through, buss her ass, and roll.

She offered me something to eat, but I ate already, so I tapped the spot next to me for her to sit. Instead of doing that, she straddled my lap. The moment she did that, I got right the fuck up, dropping her ass. This was the first time I ever smelled some raunchy shit from her.

"What's wrong?" Her face was so confused, but mine mirrored hers. I was just as confused my damn self.

"Yo, go wash that pussy now, bruh. Fuck it smell like that for?"

Embarrassment flashed almost immediately as her pecan colored skin turned red. Shit, I was embarrassed for her ass. She slowly got up and went to tend to that lobster tank. I ain't even stick around; she had blown my shit. It will be a nice minute before I come back through.

That's the worst shit you could ever do. Have smelly pussy but flaunt that shit around a nigga. I don't know about other mafuckas, but I can't get down with that shit! My car purred as I started her up. With no destination in mind, I drifted off to my spot I chill at called La'cinta. It was one of those places where you can be comfortable. The food was popping, and I even had a favorite bartender. Shit was expensive, but so was my taste. I had bread, I just knew how to stack it.

When I wanted to exude money, then I did, but on a regular day, I can easily be mistaken for a regular nigga. And that was cool, I'll smack anybody with my checkbook. I took my seat, and the waiter brought over the usual. I pulled out my phone and internet searched. There is some interesting shit on there. To the average eye, it's bullshit. To me, it's a wealth of knowledge. I don't always feed my stomach and bank account, I feed my mind too.

"Akeem, this was sent to you by the lady over there," the waiter said, almost scared to tell me.

They knew not to bother me when I'm in thought. I looked over at the person who sent me a drink then got up with it and walked in her direction.

"Excuse me, what's ya name?"

"Rashidah."

"Well, Rashidah, do me a favor, and don't do me any favors. This gesture here might have been a friendly one on ya part, but to me it's insulting. Why would I want a woman buying me drinks? Jew!" I yelled, never taking my eyes off lil momma.

"Yes, Akeem."

"Wateva this young lady is drinking, bring her the bottle and put it on my tab."

"Got you," she answered and walked off.

I did the same, leaving shawty there with a hard smirk on her face. I know y'all probably think I'm being rude, but trust me, I'm not. I'm a man first, and in my mind, a women shouldn't be sending me no damn drinks.

Chapter 8

Jequell

I left my crib and headed straight to Shyanne's spot. Shy was definitely doing too much pulling up on me like that, and she knew how I felt about her putting her hands on me. I won't hit a bitch, but I will yoke ya ass up. That was her advantage on top of the soft spot I had for her. Straight embarrassed me in front of my brothers, who dug in my ass about the shit. Even my momma had something to say about her fuck shit.

I just needed a moment to cool off, that's why I left the park. That nigga I slumped did some foul ass shit a while back, and I hadn't seen him since. Today, he was going to meet his maker if Travis ain't stop me. I was Lowkey mad he did that, but now that I'm not as fired up, I understood. I don't always think about shit, especially when it's street related and has to be dealt with. If it was on sight, then that's what it was.

At the moment, I didn't wanna deal with anybody, so I stepped off. And all this, I would have told her later, but she's so damn hardheaded and nutty. When I got there, she had the stuff I had at her house sitting outside by the door. I shook my head, leaving it right there for her to bring her ass back out there and put my shit back. Turned my key in the door, and it didn't work.

"What the fuck!" I know damn well her petty ass ain't changed the locks on a nigga.

See what I'm saying when I say she be doing way too much? It wasn't even that deep for her to do all this, and that fast too. I went around back and pulled on the window so hard the lock popped open. Climbing my big ass through it, I found her in the room talking shit to her friend about what happened earlier.

"Hang the phone up, Shyanne."

I scared the shit out of her because her words got caught in her throat.

When she did find her voice, the first thing she said was, "How you get in here, Jequell?"

I crossed the room and snatched her phone, hanging it up on the broad. I pulled my shirt off and sat at the edge of the bed. She didn't know how to take me right now, so she sat staring at me quiet as a church mouse. After gathering my thoughts, I turned around and looked at her ass. I could see her light trembles. All that mouth, and now look at her.

That's why I don't take that shit seriously when she's spazzing. It's a joke to me, but my brothers think it's something deeper every time she does it.

"The fuck you change the locks for, Shyanne?"

"Because I'm done with you. I'm tired of you treating me like I ain't shit and don't mean shit to you. I know what we have and how you feel about a "relationship," but still, stop doing the extra shit acting like you my man then. Let me go find one who wants to be with me, one who wants to go places and not have something to say about it. One who would never just up and leave and not say anything or answer his phone." Finally, she took a breath after running all that bullshit down to me.

"Shyanne, you not going anywhere, and say some more shit about getting a man, and I'll split ya fucking face," I said with fire in my eyes.

I ain't like the sound of that. I wish another nigga would think he can slide up in that or take her heart. I'll kill her and him. I don't give a fuck. She got up huffing and slamming things around. I kind of felt bad that I was holding her back from seeing other people, knowing I wasn't ready to fully commit.

Getting up off the bed, I closed the space between us. She had tears rolling down her cheeks. Shit broke me up. This was the very thing I was afraid of doing. Hurting her. But I was still doing that very thing.

"Shy, don't cry. You know how I feel about you. I know you prolly feeling like it's not enough anymore, but you been rocking this long. Just a lil more time, baby, please. My fault about earlier. I was steaming about some shit and needed to clear my head."

I lifted her face to look at me, and I could see the pain she carried. I really did want to be with her, a nigga was just scared of committing.

"I hear you, Jequell," was all she said before she pulled the covers back and got in bed.

I took the rest of my shit off and got in behind her. I just held her for the rest of the night. This was definitely where I wanted to be, it was just hard to admit that shit. Although my mom raised us to the best of her ability, I still had trust issues with giving my heart away. I do love Shyanne, I think I do, I just never told her so. Expressing that shit was more important to me, and I believe I did that very well. I didn't see the big deal about saying the actual words or even putting titles on shit.

Chapter 9

Rashidah

I heard the place to be was La'cinta, and I had to try it out for myself. With the tightest dress on that my body could stand and the baddest pair of pumps I owned, I went there by my lonely. I was on a mission, and this place was the first stop. The drinks were flowing, and I was feeling damn good. In the midst of tilting my glass up to my mouth, my eyes caught an image that made me smile. I had the bartender make a drink then asked the waiter to send it over.

The lil stunt I pulled was done purposely for a reaction. And a reaction I got. The air around him as he came over to me had me squeezing my thighs together. He was so masculine and manly. From his walk alone, I just knew he was packing a real meat package in his pants. He checked the shit out of me, and then bought me a bottle. I could do nothing but smirk at him. Everything they said he was, he is.

I got up and swayed my hips from side to side effortlessly toward him. I ain't want no smoke, I mean, not yet anyway. I just wanted to see if I could get past this lil' mix up.

"I want to apologize if I offended you. I just saw something that made my eye twinkle, so the first thing that came to mind was to send you a drink. Please, let me make it up to you," I offered

"You good, no need to make it up, sweetheart. Be careful and not sorry."

I nodded my head, getting more turned as he bossed up on my ass.

"Since you bought me this bottle, care to join me in drinking it?"

He stopped doing what he was doing and gave me his undivided attention. I thought I saw a hint of annoyance. I ain't never annoyed a nigga, damn. His eyes traveled from my toes up to my head and then back to my face directly in my eyes.

"Dig this, I got that bottle for you. I'm not interested in drinking with you. So, enjoy yaself like you were doing before I arrived. Better yet, just pretend I'm not here, love, it will be easier." He winked, got up, then dropped five benji's down on the table before walking around me and out the door.

I felt dumb as hell still standing there holding the bottle in my hand. After I picked my beak up off the floor, I was right behind him out the door. He got in this souped up charger that growled when he turned it on. I stepped back so he wouldn't see me standing there watching him.

I blew out a tired breath as I hopped in my own car and headed home. I didn't even know how to feel about what had just happened. Niggas usually fall to my feet when they see me, but Akeem was a totally different breed of a man. He was far from impressed. Shiiid, maybe even disgusted with my ass. I climbed out my wheel and entered the house where my sisters sat eating and watching TV.

"You back already?"

"I know. That was fast."

"What happened, Shidah?"

I kicked off my shoes and pulled my dress down, leaving on just my bra and thong. Neatly, I folded my dress and took a seat next to Nia.

"That nigga served my ass up a dose of bitch bye, try another nigga," I told them and tucked my feet under my butt.

"What, bitch! You the hottest thing smoking, and he played you?" Camill asked in shock.

I just shook my head and reached for the peanuts on the table.

"What now, then?" questioned Simone.

I hadn't even thought about a plan B, because I just knew he would see me and bite on it. I pondered on it, and a light bulb clicked on.

"In the meantime, Nia, you go after the Hasan character. He is the other only one who is single, and both of y'all are dumb nutty. I will still work on Akeem. Just got to come up with a better strategy, that's all."

I forgot to introduce myself. I'm Rashidah, oldest of all my siblings. Our parents had all girls, and we are the SHIT! But we also aren't SHIT either. All of us have been in love once, some twice, and it just didn't work out. So, I came up with a plan two years ago to set niggas up and rob they ass. During one of our robberies, shit went left, leaving us no choice but to dead niggas. It had been super easy up until now.

I ain't never had a nigga talk to me all crazy or do the shit Akeem did today. And though I had heard about the way he is and how he gets down, seeing it up close fucked my head up just a tiny bit. But that shit didn't last long, I'm a Henderson! And my daddy was that nigga. That was until some young niggas took his life a few years ago, leaving my mom to struggle taking care of us. Down to the last dollar or piece of bread, we've seen it all, felt it all, been through it all, which leads us to today, the attitudes, the mindsets, and the way we carry ourselves. Love don't live here anymore.

Only thing that excites us is the way a tough nigga begs for his life right before we snatch his soul. You see, we weren't always this way. At one time, we were the normal young girls looking for a man to take care of us because that's what we saw our father do with our mom. She never had to work a day in her life until it was a must that she go out and get something. Our dad was Dominican and black, and our mom was Puerto Rican and black, leaving us looking exotic and stacked in all the right places.

None of us have kids, and the way our life is set up, we made a pact to keep it that way.

Chapter 10

Hasan

The damn bugs were sticking to my front bumper and fucking up the cocaine white, so I took my car to get cleaned. I was bussing it up with my mans, BJ, when this crazy, super, stupid, dumb, thick baby slid out of a Benz coupe.

"I say, got damn, bro," BJ said with his mouth broke over mommie. I ain't gon' lie, she was all that and then some. Her head turned our way, and she winked at me.

"Aww, shit, nigga, that was all you need right there. She wants you, Has."

She was bad, but I was never the thirsty type. If she wanted a nigga, then she would walk her turkey thighs over and speak up. I waved BJ off and went back to chopping it up with him.

"Excuse me, sorry for interrupting y'all conversation, but I'm Nia. I couldn't help but notice how tall you are. It was always something about them tall guys that distracted me."

BJ and I locked eyes then I looked back at her.

"That's what's up, Nia. So, what can I do for you?" I asked her with my arms crossed over my chest.

She licked her lips and put her hand out. I looked at her manicured nails then back up to her face with uncertainty.

"You asked what can you do for me, and I'm showing you. But you have to give me ya phone in order to do that."

I took out my phone but didn't hand it to her. She just read the number off and told me to use it. As she walked away, she knew we were watching, so she put an extra bounce in her walk.

"If you don't use it, I damn sure will."

Since my mans was anxious to see what's up, I passed off the number to him. Seemed like he would appreciate it more. Once my car was finished, I peeled out, blowing one down for the ride. Since I hit that lick, I had been chilling for the most part. Then bro hit us with the bitches sticking up niggas. Now, I really don't trust a soul. Even lil momma back there had me looking at her sideways, like is it you, bitch?

I ain't putting shit past anybody. A cute face will be the main down fall, and I'll be damned if I let that happen to me or any of my brothers. Tonight, I was hitting the streets, though. Travis and Quell said they were sliding with me, so I went home and found something light but fly to put on. I wasn't a flashy nigga, but I had hot shit for days to stunt in. Since we were so known, I definitely ain't step out looking any way but edible. When a bitch sees me, she thinks I'm a piece of chocolate, and when a nigga sees me, they counting my pockets. My line was already fresh, but I called up Akeem to see if he could fix my shit up for me. Shitty sharp is the aim.

"Yo."

"Bro, can you fix me up? You know I got to be precise."

"Nigga, I just cut ya ass the other day, but I'll fall through since I'm out anyway"

"On the hood!"

Mafuckas probably thought bro was mean and ignorant. You just got to know the man to understand his logic. A few minutes later, I stepped out the shower, and this nigga was sitting on my couch fucking some grapes up.

"Ain't even gon' ask how you got in here. It's fucked up you know the codes to our shit but won't let nobody know yours"

He shrugged and got up then turned the clippers on. I sat down and let him do his thing. By the time he was finished, a nigga was feeling good. You know how girls be when they got their hair freshly done. Even an ugly bitch will have the highest self-esteem. Yeah, that's how I felt. On a high right now.

"Where y'all niggas going again?"

"Bottles Up, why? You rolling? You never go, crim. Damn, breathe a lil," I told him.

"I might. If I do, I'll meet y'all there."

I took that instead of saying anything else. He let himself back out the way he came in, and I finished getting dressed. All brown Timb's on and some light wash Hudson jeans, a Louis V button up with the print around the color, and a belt to match. One single gold chain graced my neck, and a phat ass Rollie on my arm, I was ready to go!

I sprayed a lil Bleu de Chanel on and hopped in my bitch. I scooped up Quell from crazy ass Shy's Crib. He got in, and we slapped hands.

"Sup, bro. What's the game plan tonight, though?"

"Aww man, same ol' shit, just a different night. You already!"

Travis texted and said he was pulling up in five. We were right behind him. The only thing we knew how to do was fuck shit up, then leave.

Bypassing the line, we slapped hands with Big Tank at the door. He was head of security and let us take our straps in on some just in case type shit. To show our appreciation, we all slid him a deuce a piece. You take care of us, and we take care of you.

Monica led the way to the spot that was reserved just for us. We ain't have to be knee deep in the drug game to be treated like kings. We are them niggas regardless. I slapped her ass and blew her a kiss. She rolled her eyes and continued to open our bottles and placed them back on ice.

Monica and I tried to do the serious thing a while back, but it ain't work for other reasons. Now she acted like she couldn't stand me, but I knew I could call her ass up on any given day and beat that box up. She knew it too, that's why she was always fronting.

Quell was the first to snatch up a bottle and take it to the head. Trav was gone off the good good, and this fool was banging on niggas. I laughed, taking my own bottle and joined him. I was so on point and ready for whatever this night brings.

I smiled seeing Akeem enter in bossed up. Bro might throw on some buck 90's here and there, sneaks too. But his preference is a clean shoe. Tonight, that's exactly how he was feeling. I knew his ass was gon' fall through. I heard it in his voice when he asked.

We all slapped hands with him just as Monica was bringing us more bottles. She must have seen him enter. Her tips were going to be colossal tonight. We partied and bullshitted, not having a care in the world. I mean, that's what life is about, right?

"Hey handsome," the baby from the car wash said to me, standing outside our section.

I took a swig of my drink and spoke back, "Sup, you following me?"

She laughed, and I saw her deep ass dimples. Interesting.

"Not at all, my friend is having a party tonight," she said, pointing to a group of all baddies. She waved at all my brothers, and surprisingly, they all waved back. "You be cool, Nia."

I winked at her and turned back around. She wanted to be the bitch I hang on all night, but I was smooth. Actually, I ain't even need one. I was straight right there with the bros.

Chapter 11

Travis

On the way to the club, I smoked all facials, so right now my light skin ass was zooted! Fuck drinking, I had my lean, I ain't even need nothing else. Plus, since all these niggas were steady throwing bottles back, I had to be the semi-sober one. Anything is liable to pop off, and I was gon' be the first to handle it. Emana was tryna come out with me, and any other time I wouldn't have minded. I just knew how these nights get down in a setting like this, and the last thing I wanted or needed was for her to get hurt.

If you looked hard enough, you would see the butt of my gun along with Quell's. We had big shit tucked in our pants. Akeem and Hasan had civil shit that will still twist ya body up. Some lil honey walked over smiling hard as shit in Has' face. Even though I had a girl at home, it didn't stop me from looking. And baby girl was damn sure a looker.

"Sheesh, Has, who the fuck is that?" I asked with my head tilted, watching the way one butt cheek was heavier than the other but still big and healthy.

"Right, Trav, who is it?" Quell inquired right along with me.

"Some broad who wanna get fucked," Akeem answered, watching her too.

"She most definitely wanna get fucked, bro, but I ain't give her much play. I even passed off to BJ."

We clowned on his ass for doing that. BJ wouldn't know the first thing of what to do with that.

The rest of the night, we turned this shit up to the max. All the biddies wanted to come over and party with us. Some we allowed, and others we turned away. I wasn't trying to be too crowded out. And these bitches were drinking all our shit up. I was convinced they came out with no damn money. As the club was coming to a close, I rounded up the guys. Has was lit, but Quell was the worst. Akeem and I walked behind them, watching anything moving.

The lil honey from earlier walked in front of Has and grabbed his dick. He didn't see it was her, and had we not stopped him, that bitch would have been clipped. "Bro, chill, lil baby giving you the come fuck invitation doing that," I told him, but in the condition he in, I wouldn't ever let him slip off with a random bitch or anybody for that matter.

Since they drove in the same car, we left it there. Has wasn't too happy about that, claiming he could drive, but I assured his goofy ass we would be back to get his shit in the morning.

I hit the crib to find Emana still up in the living room curled up with a blanket.

"Should have known you were going to still be up."

"I wasn't closing my eyes until you got here," she said matter-of-factly.

Sneering at her, I picked her up and carried her to the room. She wrapped her arms around my neck at the same time, placing her head there too. I gave her two quick pecks to the forehead and told her that I loved her. Mana reached down and pulled the covers back. Once I placed her in bed, I took a quick a shower to wash the events of the night off.

As I turned the water off to get out, she was standing right there with one leg on the sink showing that bare face pussy. I bricked up on sight. I walked over to her, Johnson stiff as a mafucka. Our tongues locked, and I eased my way into her wet ass box. She was leaking so much that my dick was coated in juices. I took my time giving out long deep strokes, all while holding her leg up. I was still lit up, so I wasn't in a rush to get this nut off.

Her shit was squeezing my dick. I had to pull out and think of bananas to slow myself down from cuming. Emana loved the way I handled her sweet gushy. Every time, I aimed to please with her. The bathroom wasn't letting me get up in there like I wanted to, so I spread her ass out on the bed and plowed her. She was screaming, scratching, shouting, and I loved every minute of it.

She flipped the script when she started to throw it back at me. It was a losing battle then. Down went the fuck Frazier! I tensed up and grabbed her hair with one hand then her neck with the other. I landed sloppy, wet kisses on her lips while I shot off inside of her.

"Ugh, wait, don't pull it out yet, baby."

I never knew what was with her not wanting me to pull out right after. If I ain't know any better, I would think she wanted a nigga's baby. I let my dick jump and pulsate inside of her as we lay there sweating and breathing hard.

All that shit I smoked was catching up to me because I fell asleep right in the pussy with my mouth wide open.

Chapter 12

Akeem

Nobody was cooking today, and I got tired of spending my money on fast food. I was at the market half-baked right now tryna figure out what I wanted to cook that wouldn't take long. Stuck between chicken and fish, I stood in the middle of the aisle with both in my hand.
"You should get the fish." I looked to my left, and there was that chick again from La'cinta's
"Oh yeah?"
"Yup, I could tell you a few ways to make it. Wait, you are the one cooking it right?" she questioned with an eyebrow raised.
I finally got a good look at her, and she was thick as grits.
"You nosey, but yeah."
She giggled at me saying she was nosey. For some reason, she looked like somebody, I just couldn't figure out who. I put the chicken back and grabbed the fish. She took that as an invitation to walk with me around the store getting other things I needed. Since I wasn't a man of too many words, she did the most talking. Trying every now and then to ask me questions that I barely gave up answers to.

I kept a neutral face as I paid for my stuff. I told her good looking for her ideas and bounced. I knew she was bloody about that, but she sneaky weird, crim. And that, I don't like. But I did go home and master the lil recipe she gave me. Shit was hyphy too. I ain't save any. A lil later, I stepped out to collect some more bread I had out there. I know y'all probably trying to figure out what I do. I'm a loan shark.

I loan out money to those who need it right away, and in return, I put interest on it. Majority of the people know not to play with me and they have my shit right. But then you have the ones like Van, who thought they could shake me and lay low. I find niggas, I always do when it comes to my money, and I don't discriminate. If you need money, I got you. Just don't play pussy and get fucked.

Since I had a few hours to burn, I hit the gym up. I did have a few things at the crib to work out with, but it was something about being in a gym setting that I liked better. Call it competition, but if I see somebody else getting it in as hard as me, I secretly challenge them in my head. That's how I stay motivated and on my shit.

I showered the sweat away, threw on my 'go get it' attire, and dipped. Walking or riding a bike was more my thing when it came down to making moves. I sometimes felt like cars can get in the way of getting away. A car can't fit through an alley or a tight spot. I leaned against the back of an abandoned truck that was parked in this yard.

It really pissed me off when I had to get my hands dirty because somebody thought it was okay to toy with my emotions. And it didn't matter who you were, if you were bold enough to take money from me, then you were bold enough to be dealt with if you didn't pay up.

Lidia entered her crib from the back like I thought she would, not even paying attention to her surroundings. I was glad to see she didn't have her kid with her because I don't do kids.

Creeping up behind her, I didn't give her a chance to shut the door all the way before I jumped inside with her. She fell against the table, knocking shit over. I stood there staring down at her ass, starting to get mad. She was a beautiful woman, would make any man happy, but today she made me mad as hell. I was not the bad guy in this situation. She knew what would happen if she didn't fall through, and I gave her extra time.

"Akeem, baby, I was going to call you today. I have half of it," she tried pleading with me.

"Go get it, and try anything, you already know what will happen."

She got up slowly and went into a jar sitting on top the refrigerator. I counted what she had, and it was half the money, but that wasn't gon' get it for me.

"Please, I just need a few more days. I can make it up to you, I mean just to hold off."

I still stood in the same spot, not moved by her tactics. She started taking her clothes off and walking over to me. She got on her knees and pulled on my pants until my dick popped out. Wrapping her thick lips around my shit, she sucked until I was brick. I let her do her thing because her head was definitely fire. And right after I bussed down her throat, I took out my knife and slit hers.

You could never play me with pussy. I wasn't a sucka ass nigga in desperate need. I'm a business man, and if you can't treat me as such, then I'll show you. I left back out the way I came, making sure my hand print wasn't on anything.

Chapter 13

Hasan

BJ was over my crib eating all my shit up on some high shit. I ain't mad though, I barely ate, especially here.

"Yo, I'm about to call the babe from the car wash up," he said all hype like she gave his ass the number.

I shrugged, took a seat, and sparked my own shit up. This nigga had the nerve to FaceTime shawty. I shook my head at this clown.

"Who are you and how you get my number? Better yet, why are you Facetiming me?"

I cracked up laughing because she just went in on this nigga.

"You don't remember giving me ya number a couple days ago?"

"Fuck no! I only gave my number to one person, and I know damn well it wasn't you!"

"Calm down, baby. We can get to know each other since I got you on the phone."

"No the fuck we can't either. Where is the tall guy you were with?"

"Oh, so you do remember me then?"

"Nigga, like I said, I didn't give my number to you, I gave it to him. So where the fuck he at!?"

I was laughing so hard, my damn stomach started to hurt. That bitch was crazy. Just my type.

BJ flipped me the bird and threw his phone at me. I picked it up and puffed on my shit.

"Hey sexy, why you playing games and shit?"
I blew the smoke out. "I don't play games, sweetheart. And you ain't have to talk to my mans like that. He was interested, and we don't step on each other toes over here," I told her.
She sucked her teeth and rolled her eyes. Called herself going off on me too, but I cut that shit short. Told her watch her damn mouth. I'm a grown ass man and I'll take my belt off and beat her big, round ass.
She thought that shit was funny, but I wasn't playing. You can't talk to me any ol' kind of way and get away with it. Bitch or not. I found myself on the phone with her until BJ's battery died. He was sick at me. Didn't even mean for that to happen. Nia was cool people. I told her we could go for some drinks or something later on. I was tryna fuck since she acted like that's what she wanted anyway. So, if I had to buy her ass a drink, I didn't mind. She was a lil classier then the skeeze buckets that flock this way. Going to the liquor store the first time linking up wouldn't fly with her. After BJ charged his phone, he dipped off, talking shit about me going out with his future wife. I wasn't feeding into his bullshit. The way she came at him, he wouldn't even be able to handle her mouth, let alone that phat ass. I called my bro bro Akeem up and told him about me sliding off with Nia. I always felt comfortable when I knew he knew the last person I was with.

A nigga like myself don't go out with females anyhow, but she insisted on seeing me. Since I wasn't doing shit, I didn't mind. But that don't change the fact that I don't trust her ass as far as I can throw her. Akeem told me to go and have a grown time. Said I'm always fucking around with these nothing ass bitches, but if I feel like the babe ain't right, take her to the back of the parking lot and dump a few in her.

I was with that; the smallest thing can make me nervous. Any wrong move or even words on her part could seal her fate tonight.

Chapter 14

Nia

I was finally able to get a chance to meet up with this Hasan character. The nigga was playing hard to get like he ain't like every groove he saw on my body. Not too many people have my number, and I really did only give it out to him that day, so when the number flashed for a call, I automatically thought it was him. But the face that was on my screen wasn't his ass, and I got annoyed as hell.

I knew the dude was the one who was standing out there with him, but I still couldn't understand for the life of me why he was calling me and not Hasan. Then talking that bullshit 'bout getting to know each other. Like, nigga, hell nah! This shit here doesn't work like that. I got standards, and he was definitely not even close to those.

"What did he say, Nia?" Rashidah asked me as I entered back into the room where they all were.

I didn't want him to see my background, so I got up and answered the phone in my room.

"We going for some drinks tonight."

"Bitch, don't get cute."

"Girl bye, this is a job, not a social call," I reminded her.

I'm the sister that when we ain't doing shit, I like to go out and have a normal life. This shit here is not all it's cracked up to be. Yes, our life went from sugar to shit, and I did at one point let it get to me. But now, I'm 24, and it didn't hurt to act like a normal 24-year-old.

"Y'all chill out. She doing more than any of us are doing right now. Just stay focused, Nia, and we will be good," Rashidah said.

I nodded my head, only half caring about what she was saying. They were always on my ass, yet I get the job done every time. I may do some shit out of whack, but I just do things my way. I don't see what the big deal is if the end result is it's done.

I excused myself and went back up to my room to find something cute to wear. I knew Camille had something to say, and I didn't give a fuck! She better watch me work! That's it, that's all! Oh, and for the record, I'm the baby of my sisters. I took it the hardest when my father was killed because I was a daddy's girl. He gave me anything and everything I wanted, which is why I think sometimes I butt heads with my sisters.

They would always complain about how I got away with shit that they would get in trouble for. And I would stick my tongue out and tease them. That shit really never died because now Rashidah still treats me as a baby and spoils me. Simone and Camille hate it. My mommy even still acts the same with me. Speaking of her, I have to drop in and give her some money. Now that we were baller bitches, she didn't need to buss her ass working anymore. We put her up in a nice ass house where she had a maid. Although what we did didn't bother her, she did stay on us about changing our lifestyle and having some kids. Our pact was to never have kids. At least not any time soon.

I found a sexy ass red jumper to wear. It was shorts and had diamonds for the straps. I put on a silver crop top to pop the look along with some bad ass Loub's to match. Since I didn't have the patience to really do my hair, I twisted it up in a bun, leaving a few strands to hang. The way my legs and thighs looked in this, I knew his ass was gon' drip at the mouth at least once, if not twice tonight.

I gathered up everything I needed including my baby 9.

"Oh bitch!" Simone said, watching me walk through.

"Kill 'em, baby," Rashidah added.

"You look real nice, Nia," Camille commented with a wink.

We weren't always at each other necks, and when we weren't, that's we were at our best. I told them I would give them a text if I needed back up, but I truly didn't think I would. I was a bad bitch with this gun.

Chapter 15

Jequell

I was mad as shit that my ma had me helping her redo the crib. She had three other sons, yet she woke me up out my sleep for this shit. This was why half the time I stayed with Shy. I had just got in like four hours ago, and I was tired as shit.

"Stop slamming my shit around, lil nigga. If ya ass wasn't out all times of the night, then you wouldn't have to worry about being sleepy."

"Ma, I'm grown, though."

"Yeah, and ya grown ass lives right here with me, ya momma. So, all that grown shit doesn't fly this way. Now pick this up and take it to the curb for me."

I grumbled, almost snatching the table up for her. She stopped and gave me the evil eye, like *I dare you*. I wasn't in the mood to get hit with anything she picked up, so I got the shit and took it outside.

As I was walking back in, some nigga tried to run up on me. I saw him coming and hit this nigga with a quick, stiff one. Knocked his dumb ass cold out. I used my boots to stomp the nigga head into the ground. The gun he had slipped out of his hand, and I picked it up to pop his shit, but my ma screamed at me.

"Jequell! Don't you fucking dare do that shit in front of my house! Call ya brothers to come help you now!"

I hit this nigga few more times to make sure he was out, and dragged his ass to the basement. By the time I got upstairs, my ma had already called them. I threw a shirt on and a hoodie. The nigga had a mask on, and I hadn't even taken it off him yet.

All my brothers came through the door on go time a couple minutes later.

"Where he at?" Has asked, ready to get busy

"Basement," I said, leading the way.

When we got down there, ol' boy was trying to crawl back out the door, but I fucked him up pretty badly. He could barely move. Trav grabbed the back of his jacket and dragged him back to the middle of the floor. Hasan snatched his mask off, and I chuckled at the sight before me.

"Wow, so this this nigga had the balls to come after me. See, Trav, you should have let me kill his ass the first time."

"Well, now you can, bro."

"What, you know this nigga?" Akeem questioned, stroking his beard.

"Yeah, this the clown he was fucking up at the park who he almost killed out there, but I stopped him."

"Solid. Welp it's time to handle this bitch!"

Has picked up a sledge hammer that was lying around and cracked this nigga's skull. I just heard the bones in his head break. We didn't want to shoot our guns off in the basement of our ma's crib, so we beat his ass to death.

Once I knew he was a goner, I dragged him back outside and to the big dumpsters at the end of the block. We weren't worried about anybody seeing what we were doing. They knew better than to speak on shit. It was nothing to run off up in somebody's crib and lay they ass down. Mind your business, and you live to see another day. They stuck around for a few to make sure nothing else was popping off. I was glad because after all that, she made us all help redo the crib.

One thing about ma, she didn't pay about her boys. She knew we were far from saints, and she accepted that.

Chapter 16

Me and my pop were playing ball on the court in front of his crib. I had been missing in action a few days, so I stopped by today to see what his old ass was up to. We got to talking shit back and forth about who can beat who, so I challenged him to a game. My pop was in good shape and still had a crazy hand on the ball, but he wasn't better than me. I beast shit.

The type of relationship we had, it was like we were more brothers then son and dad. Aside from my ma and brothers, he was really there for me throughout my whole life. I appreciated him for not abandoning me. Shiid, sometimes I think him and my ma' still be getting it in. She always gets to smiling when she asks about my pop. And when I call her out on it every time, she just says that he's her friend.

"Ahh!" I yelled, making a slam dunk that won the game.

"I let you have that," my pop said.

"Aww, come on with the bullshit, Pop. I had you."

"Yeah, yeah, so what's up with you? Where you been?"

"Just working, chilling and shit. You know the same ol' same ol.'"

"I hope so. They say they found a body out there near ya mom crib. Be careful over there. I know you and ya brothers be having y'all hands on shit."

"Pops, I'm good, we good. How about you, though? You good? Everything straight around here? You need some money or something?"

He laughed and waved me off. I knew if he did, he would never tell me or ask me. That was just how he was. But it never hurt to throw it out there that I had him if he did need me. Shiid, nowadays, he was getting old despite his looks, and it was time to chill a lil. He still worked for the infirmary. Been there since I was a youngin'. Let him tell it, he will never leave until he can't move a muscle.

That game had me starving, so Pop ordered us some pizza. I sat and ate that with him while talking more shit. I loved this time with him. The bond we had was a tight one, and I wouldn't trade this shit here for nothing.

Pops knew what my brothers and I can get into, but even with the way we are, I still wouldn't tell him anything about what we do. As for that nut nigga, he deserved everything he got that night. Can't run up on any of us and live to tell about it. Nah, shit don't move that way.

It was night fall by the time I left my pop's crib. Emana had hit me a few times just wondering what I was doing. I didn't mind, though. As long as she wasn't tripping on me, we were straight.

And like any other time, she was waiting for me when I got in. I loved that she did that, but I had told her plenty times that she didn't have to, especially when I knew I was going to be long or coming in late. Either way, she still wasn't trying to hear that.

"How was ya dad, baby?"

"His young old ass is good. My body gon' be sore tomorrow fooling around with him."

"You want me to rub you down tonight, so you will be good in the morning? You said you got to work a few extra hours, right?"

Oh shit! I forgot all about that. My boss asked me to work another shift since they were going to be short, and I agreed just thinking about the money. But sitting there, I was sick thinking about it.

"Damn, bae, I'm glad you reminded me. I truly forgot, fuck! Ard, yeah. I need a rub down."

I hopped up before I started to get too lazy and hit the water. My baby was waiting for me as soon as I got out with the body rub. It has some type of soothing feeling to it. Every time I play ball, she hooks me up. This was where I felt old as hell. Can't ball without my body feeling like a mac truck hit me the next day. On the hood.

Chapter 17

Hasan

I was out on my lil date or whatever you want to call it with Nia when my mom called me yelling about Jequell was about to kill somebody out front of the house. I barely got out that I would get at her later before I dipped, and haul tailed it to the crib. When you say the word KILL to me, all total sense goes out the window, and in walks Mr. Heartless. It didn't take me long to reach my ma's crib because I took all back streets.

Bro was on his way down to the basement where some nigga was trying to escape. I didn't know the clown, and at this point, that shit didn't really matter. We beat his ass into a permeant sleep and dragged him down the street. My night was cut short, but I made sure my brothers were good and slid off. I was having a smooth time with the shawty. Since my attitude was on 'fuck you, pay me' I called her back up and told her to meet me at the smash spot.

She had been wanting to throw that ass in a roundabout, and I wasn't gon' let it waste. I got there a few minutes before she did and straightened up some. Not too many nights ago, I had somebody there bent over the couch screaming bloody murder. I thought the guy downstairs was gon' come up here and fuck my shit up because she was hollering so loud. All these bitches want the dick until you whip it out, and the words they were talking get caught the fuck up in they dick suckers.

Soft but stern knocks graced the door while I was just finishing up. I washed my hands and went to open the door.

"You changed, huh?"

"I figured why not? I knew when you said crib we weren't going to be out in public, so I wanted to be chill."

I nodded, looking out behind her and scanning the area then shutting the door with the locks clicking. I could tell by her face that she wasn't impressed with the crib. But that was her business, never judge a book by its cover. Only if she knew this was like a trap house, but with no drugs other than smoke sacks.

We used this spot for leisure anyhow, and I have never brought a bitch to my own crib. It's too secret of a place, and on top of me being paranoid, I could never sleep comfortable. My brothers, ma, and my only man know where I stay. I'd like to keep it that way.

"So, this is where you sleep?"

I looked at her, trying read her from that comment. When I didn't answer, she turned to me and shifted her weight as she tilted her head. I thought the lil gesture was cute, but she was being smart about it.

"Maybe, why?"

"I'm just asking. The kind of car you have and from what I've seen, I just figured ya crib would be strapped too."

And there you have it. Now I would be the bad guy for thinking she a gold digging bitch, right?

"What does it matter? You looking for a sponsor or a good time?"

She smirked as she took off her jacket. Them full D cups bounced out while her flat stomach was on display. And the damn jeans she had on, I know her coochie was suffocating in there. They were so tight, her pussy print was on camel toe.

"The fuck? You had to lay across the bed to get ya pants on?"

She started laughing hard as shit.

"No, dumb ass. They stretch, so I pulled them up regularly. You crazy. Anyway, what's to eat here?

"Damn, you still hungry?"

"Hasan, did you or did you not forget that you just rushed out after that phone call? What, you thought I was gon' sit there by myself all night looking stupid? I didn't eat, nigga. Now is there any food here to eat?"

I just stared at her for a minute. Wasn't sure if I wanted to tell her watch her mouth or blow her a kiss. I waved her over to the kitchen. I barely ever cook there, but I always have food. I would rather order take out if I got hungry, but now that she mentioned something, a nigga was definitely starving outchea, crim.

After showing her that it was all frozen shit in there, she pulled out some steaks to thaw out in water. While that was thawing, she took some potatoes, cut them up, tossed them around in a pan with seasoning. I stood back and watched her every move. Her back side was crazy, but just seeing how she whipped up a quick meal had me looking at her ass slightly different. The food was good as shit. I barely swallowed it; steak was tender as hell.

I had all the intentions of bussing her ass and never calling again. She had changed that scenario, though. Her conversation was flowing. She would be geeked up off me, and had comebacks for days. I even started to pass off hot ones, but she in turn lit my ass up too. By the time we thought about looking at a clock, it was three in the morning. My desire to fuck was heightened, but I still didn't push the issue.

Here is the thing. You have to be liked in some kind of way for any of my brothers or I to fuck you more than once. And, like I said, she was gon' get this dick and gone 'head somewhere. But since she actually had me chillin' regular with her ass, she can stay around for another link up. I got comfortable on one couch and she did the other. It was a battle for both of us to stay up, I was getting tired as shit, but tired or not, I wasn't going to sleep before she did. And I slept with one eye open.

Any time she moved, I had my hand on my gun, ready to shoot her ass. Luckily, around 8 ish, her phone started dancing with calls and texts back to back. I started to think she had a nigga, and he realized she ain't bring her ass back home last night. She read my mind because she said it was her sister who was worried about her. Once she was in her car and down the road, I locked up, went out the back, and walked over a few blocks to my crib.

I dragged myself in there to shower then hit the bed. Only thing about living in the streets is you could never get too comfortable. My black ass be spent some days. This here and my ma's crib are the only places you will really catch me with my guard down. But that doesn't mean my gun isn't on safety, and I'm not on point.

Chapter 18

Rashidah

The day I ran into Akeem at the market and he actually gave up a small conversation, I thought maybe I had him. But again, he played me to the left. I was starting to question myself on my skills. It had just become a major challenge that I was not about to back down from. If it took me months, then so be it. Now, it wasn't just all about setting his ass up anymore, shit just got personal.

Normally, I wouldn't put the word personal with anything I do as far as work related. And that's because it hasn't ever taken me this long to get close to a nigga. His ass was just a tough nail that didn't wanna go in the wall, but eventually, they all do. My only thing is, if I can't approach him the way I have done, then I got to be a lil more nonchalant towards him. But shiid, how the fuck am I to do that when he barely looks my way? I really tried to pry shit out of him that day, but he gave answers to what he wanted and said nothing to some. Just gave me a weird look like he didn't trust my ass at all. And that's fine, I wouldn't trust my fine ass either. I lowkey liked this cat and mouse game. It was intriguing. I hadn't put my other two sisters on the other two yet. From what I know, they probably wouldn't give either of them the time of the day because of the loyalty they carried for their bitches.

It's no biggie anyhow. The main one we want is Akeem. Well, more so who I want. We had some insight on some other niggas, and that is who Simone and Camille have been getting at. Akeem came across my radar in the midst. I, on the other hand, wanted to be the one to get his ass, and when he played me like an Xbox, I had to have him. Putting Nia onto Hasan was just an extra bonus.

Nia thinks I don't peep that she really doesn't want to this shit anymore. But that's my baby sister, and I know everything there is to know about her. She is young, and she wants to do shit other bitches her age are doing. I get that, but it's not an option. I mean, at least for now it's not. I knew giving her something to do would keep her busy for a while. As ruthless as I am, Nia is probably right under me, if not better.

I rarely ever had to worry about her, but when she went on her date, came home so soon, then left back out, I was on edge. All she said was that she going to meet back up with the nigga. I thought that was a solid, being as though he cut the date short. I just didn't expect her to never come back. Her answering the phone sent a major relief over me. If anything was to happen to any of my sisters, I would definitely feel at fault.

I was dogged the worst by my last man; he even thought I was his punching bag until I killed his ass. The feeling I got afterward was one I couldn't explain. But all I knew was no more cheating, lying, fucking bitches in my car, in our house, no more fighting them, slicing them up over him. The beating, smacking, punishments, were all over. I didn't have to live in fear anymore or hide for weeks from my family just so they wouldn't see the bruises, black eyes, and broken ribs.

I was pregnant with twins, and this nigga one night came in smelling like a bitch with lipstick on his shirt and dried up cum in the front of his pants, drunk as hell. I went clean the fuck off, having enough of the bullshit. Then some lil bitch was playing on my phone earlier that day too. I started swinging, didn't care that he would fuck me up. I was hurt, and there was no other way to put it. When he got his bearings together, he punched me like I stole his stash and gave him AIDS.

I lost my breath after the fifth one. He then stomped me the fuck out until blood just flowed from my pussy. Right then is when I knew that if I didn't do something, he would kill me. Since I was bleeding so rapidly, I knew the babies were gone. And as much of an attachment that I had with them at five months, I was kind of glad they were gone, because what I did next would have haunted me. Seeing their smiling faces and knowing who their father was and what I went through would have been too much.

Hell, it was hell in our household. I felt like dying every day; too scared to leave, but too in love to try. The word LOVE, is so powerful, yet so fucking evil. The last time he lifted his leg to come down on me, I grabbed it and snatched him so quick, he went flying backwards. Because he was fucked up still, he lay there holding his head. I crawled to the door to get out of his way, holding on to the wall to stand up.

With the little bit of strength I had left in my body, I moved slowly to the room. My muscles were hurting, and the babies felt like they wanted to slide right out of me. Everything on my body was in pain, but that didn't stop me from making sure that I will never hurt again. I couldn't open the safe fast enough. When the locks clicked, I breathed a sigh of relief. Inside, he always kept two guns loaded. I picked up the biggest one, not sure at the time what it was. I just knew it was heavy and would do what I needed it to do.

Blood trailed behind me with every step I took, and when I reached him, he drunkenly looked up to the barrel of his own gun and tried to grabbed at it, but I pulled the trigger until it clicked, indicating that it was empty. I ran some water in the tub and lowered myself in there. Instantly, the water turned red, but the color of it was the last thing on my mind. No one was there but me and my dead ass nigga. So, I pushed. It was painful as fuck, but I wasn't stopping until they both were out of me.

And when the last one popped out, I used the scissors to cut all the placenta hanging from my body. The hard part was over. I looked down at the two lil tiny bodies lying face down in the tub and cried. That night was the last night I ever cried, and I vowed then that never will a man make me into a human punching bag. It was kill them all if I had to from there.

It took a few weeks for me to get back to normal. When my face healed up enough and my body was damn near free of bruises, I went to the hospital and made up a bullshit story about feeling lower abdominal pain. They checked me out and said that everything looked to be okay. That was all I needed to hear. Since I delivered my own babies, I wanted to make sure I didn't fuck myself up.

In the backyard of our house, I buried him along with the twins. And when the time was right, I stopped in on my mom and sisters a new woman. They were happy to see me, and I felt the same way. But ever since then, when they would say they were going through shit at home or I saw their men out doing fuck shit, I would either pop one in them for a silent warning or kill them. Eventually, they gave up on love too, and then, I introduced them to this life. Surprisingly, they adapted really quickly, especially Nia. It was like she was born for it. Many times, I had to tell her to chill because she was getting reckless and leaving a trail. So far, we are still undetected. This was a state to state business. After making out, we move out. And here is where we are now. Once Simone and Camille get their lick and I get Akeem, we will be out of here as well.

Chapter 19

Nia

Sometimes, all it takes is a lil consistency, and I made sure I stayed persistent with Hasan. I'm not gon' lie, I did think he probably wasn't gon' give me a small chance. I was super irritated that somebody called him. It sounded like a woman, and he just left me sitting there looking lonely and hungry. I went home pissed and lay across the bed, tryna figure out how I was gon' get his ass for playing me like that.

But when he called me back later saying to come over, I was happy. Once I changed, I headed right over there. I can't really tell you what I was expecting, but his spot was definitely not somewhere I thought he would live. And by his response when I did ask, it made me think that crib was a front, especially since we crashed on the couch and not in a damn bed where normal people sleep.

Whatever, though. I did get too comfortable. I don't fall asleep with niggas nowhere. But after I cooked that food and smoked with him, it was a struggle from there to keep my eyes open. I peeped him doing the same, but once I crashed, shiid, I really didn't give a shit. Rashidah gave me the business when I got back to the crib, asking me a million questions that I didn't feel the need to answer.

Because I felt like that, I gave her all bullshit. She knew it was too by the look she gave me back. Like damn, I just got on the job, I need breathing room before she jumps down my neck. I been doing this shit, I got this. And I think I got a small piece of Hasan's guard down when I showed him it was nothing to get in the kitchen and put some shit together. His body language relaxed some.

I hit a nerve when I asked him about that being his crib. Smart ass mouth, I already see he gon have me in my bag. Overall, though, he was cool people. If it was another lifetime, I would take his ass personal, but this was just business, baby. Shidah puts us on, and we execute. Never mix the two. The number one rule that can easily get you killed.

Today, we were all kind of was chilling, so I figured I'd take my talents to the nail shop and then the mall. I needed some new sneaks and boots. I wasn't much of a heel chick, but don't get it fucked up, I have plenty of them. Shit with tags still on them. I was more of a sneaker, shoe type bitch. Never know when you have to throw hands, and when I go off, ain't no time to pull shoes off. I got dressed in some distressed jeans and a plain shirt with my bomber fitted jacket along with my Chanel loafers. Real simple but cute. I have to always keep my appearance up. It just ain't in me to walk out looking all types of crazy.

"Uh, where you going?" Simone inquired, stopping me in my tracks.

"Out. Why, you wanna come?"

"Nope, be careful."

I winked at her and kept it pushing. Careful was my middle name. If I even felt like something was off, I ain't got a problem shooting me a nigga or a bitch. I walked into the nail shop with my head held the highest it could go. The whispers started along with the stares, but that was natural, and I welcomed it. Only one lady touched my nails, and she had someone in her seat. I nodded my head, letting her know I was there.

I don't sit more than ten minutes waiting. If there was somebody next, she would just have one of the other girls do them or they would wait. Not my problem. I paid crazy money for the shit I get done, probably the highest payer in this bitch. These raggedy bitches ain't have no real money. They come in there with slippers and scarfs on.

I hate that this chick could do bad ass nails, but worked there with all those unstable creatures. Wasn't even a good five minutes before she called me over and some goat looking heifer had a problem with that.

"Oh, nah ah, LiLi, I been waiting for over an hour, and she just walked in. The fuck kind of shit is going on here?"

"She appointment," LiLi told her in her broken English.

I blew a kiss at the bitch and took my seat. I asked myself if she was worth me getting out of pocket. She carried on the whole time I was in the chair, but I remained calm, appearing unbothered. A few people just kept staring at me and giving me nasty looks, but only the clown opened her mouth.

When Lili was done, I got up and paid her with a tip also, and kindly walked over to the lady. She had so much to say, but was now looking like she wasn't sure what I was about to do. I raised my hand and smacked spit right from her mouth. There were no words that needed to be said, so I walked out. But that was not the end of it. Ms. Big and Bad followed me out the shop talking big shit. My nails were fresh, and I wasn't in the mood to sit any longer if I broke one by fucking her up. I hit the locks on my car and stuck my bag and phone in there. She was walking toward me as everybody filed out the shop to be nosey. But I had a trick for this goofy hoe. When she got up real close, she went to swing. I ducked it and put my gun to her stomach. Nobody could see it but us.

"Now, I want you to turn ya dumb, pre-hype ass back around and slide right back on in the shop with them rollers on ya feet. This here, bitch, is not what you want," I said with gritted teeth.

She was scared, but also mad that she couldn't shoot her shot of showing off for those nothing ass bitches over there watching and waiting. I slowly took the gun away and smacked her ass again, sending her steaming.

So the fuck what, though? I came in minding my business, and she just had to interfere with that. Now her life was threatened, and she got slapped twice. When I felt her distance was far enough, I got in my shit and peeled. Almost fucked my mall trip up, but I'll be damn if I let that petty shit get in the way of spending money.

Nordstrom was packed, and I got irritated all over again. Fuck was all these people in there for on a Thursday? The whole time I shopped, I had my nose turned up.

"Uhm, that's not a good look, crim."

I heard the voice and stopped what I was doing. To my left stood Hasan tall as ever, but looking good, I must admit.

"Hasan, didn't expect to see you. What's up?"

"Fuck that. What's up with ya face all frowned up? I thought bitches is happy when they shopping. Unless you window shopping." He said that shit with a straight face.

I wasn't sure if I should laugh or cuss his ass out for disrespecting me like that.

"Nigga, do I look like a window shopping bitch?"

"Shiid, can't judge a book by its cover."

Okay, so now it's' safe to say he was getting under my skin. I was about to leave his ass standing right there with his assumptions. Mafuckas just want to fuck with me today.

"What's on ya to do list after this?"

I started to say none of his got damn business.

"Nothing, really. Why?"

"Slide off with me."

I was definitely sliding off with him, I just had to make it look like I wasn't interested. He didn't give me time to think because he just dipped after telling me to call him when I was ready. Ol' rude fucker.

Chapter 20

Akeem

I was racking my brain trying to figure out why I hadn't gotten any science on the bitches out there setting shit up. It was like soon as I got wind, they blew right with that mafucka. I wish I had a description on what they looked like. It's a rack of females around, and it was hard to pinpoint who the hell was who. But either way, that's why I stayed guarded. I still had ears and eyes open to the streets. I didn't stand on blocks and corners, and that was where you can come up off anything you wanted to know.

No doubt, even with not standing out there, anything they hear I hear. So, it wasn't a problem nor was I missing shit. My trust level just went from barely my own momma to damn near no one. It wasn't personal, but setting a nigga up is the ultimate worst thing you could do in my eyes. And females mess it up for the good ones who will never get a chance.

Today, I was cruising the streets just clearing my mind. A few people spoke up and others just looked. I liked to show my face every once in a while, just so they know I'm always around but just out of sight. All I saw was ass plastered in the air at the same time looking under the hood of a car. I started to just ride past, but my conscience wouldn't let me. All those clowns out there, and everybody just looking but ain't a damn soul helping. An ass like that better come with a face to match.

The hell was she doing under the hood anyway in the middle of the hood?

"What's the problem, lil momma?"

When she came out from under there, I cussed myself. Why in the hell did I keep running into this broad, man?

"Hey, I don't know. It started making a weird noise while I was driving, and I just pulled right over. I don't know shit about cars."

"For starters, what year is this?"

"Fifteen."

For her car to be a '15, it's no way it should be making any kind of noise. I knew a lil something about cars. And because I lowkey had a passion for fixing them, it was the main reason I pulled over in the first place to help her. I took a glance at everything under the hood, just giving it an eye. I hopped in and took it for a spin around the corner. Sure enough, it had a knocking sound. One that I hoped ain't have shit to do with her engine, or else that would be nutty as shit, on the hood.

"Aye, listen, this shit sounds serious. And if it's what I'm thinking, it might be ya engine. Where the fuck did you get the car from?"

"The auction."

Figures. They will sell any damn thing just to take ya money. I watched her stand there looking frustrated. I was contemplating if I wanted to help her ass. It was something about her that nagged at me, and when I feel like that, I stay the fuck away. But on another note, she looked innocent. Although, looking innocent and harmless will still get ya ass killed, I decided to help her, but it was nothing to stuff her ass in the trunk of her own car with blood leaking while I fixed the bitch. It can be her choice.

"Listen, this weekend, bring ya car to this location, and I will check deeper into it. If it's the engine, I can take you to this spot where you can get a rebuilt one, and I'll put it in for you."

Her face lit up upon hearing me say that. See, that weird shit right there. It wasn't a genuinely happy a nigga looking out smile. That bitch was full blown hype.

I just walked off on her before I changed my mind.

"Wait, how am I supposed to get in contact with you?"

I turned back around then walked back up to her. "I told you to come to this location. There is no other reason you need to contact me, Rashidah."

I fucked her head with that one, but I don't forget names or faces. I was dead ass about her not needing me until this weekend when she brings the car. Where I told her to come was a spot where I worked on cars. Yeah, ya boy is a jack of all trades. I get this money all ways, and if you didn't know me personally, then you really would think I was in the way out here, bum shit.

But, crazy part is, my money is just as long as the plug. I just choose not to slang shit but this dick when I want. She was still standing there with that 'I can't stand his ass' look on her face as I rode past her. I wasn't put on this earth to be liked, so she better get with the program.

Speaking of slanging dick, I ran down on my young mommy. She was my lil buss it baby. Strictly fucking. We barely have conversation for each other. She hit me when she wants the dick, and I hit her when I need to feel her water. And that's what I like about her. No complaint or mistaking what we have for anything else. When I'm feeling generous, I sometimes drop a few bills on her just because.

She met me at the door, closing it while cornering me and unzipping my pants. I locked eyes with her as she deep throated my shit off gun buss. She always made that shit Nasty Nancy for a nigga. Her mouth was so wet, spit was just sliding down her chin on my nuts. "Damn, Ketta," I grumbled.

That made her go harder, but I pulled her up. I didn't want to end it right there. I had the tendency to get that first one off and leave it just like that. One thing you got to learn about me is, I'm really not pressed for a bitch or the shit she possesses between her legs. That shit is out there. I focus more on money than anything else.

Jail made me this way. And yeah, I said jail. If I sat down and told you all the damn shit I got into when I was behind the walls, you wouldn't believe it. Som now, my train of thought had changed. I don't take anything for granted. With a swift move, I put my hat on and picked her lil ass up, holding her high in the air. She eased down on that big mafucka and panted. After all the times I ran up in her guts, she still wasn't used to the size.

Ketta bounced up and down with a steady pace, giving us both the satisfaction that was well needed. Feeling like if I didn't take over, this shit would be a done deal soon, I flipped her over in a handstand and squatted in that pussy.

"Akeeeeem! Guh!"

The way she said my name was so angelic. I felt like I was touching the bottom of that pussy. She was grabbing at imaginary things. One last hard, deep pump, and I pulled out and nutted in the condom. Gently, I let her down on her back where she lay. She already knew it wasn't no staying around to chill afterwards.

*****

The weekend came faster then I cared for it to. Now, I started to regret being nice. I have a way of coming off rude, yet still nice to a mafucka, and I couldn't help that to save my life. I got my swoll on, took a quick shower, then heading to the yard. Rashidah was actually there before I was. Can't say I was too happy about that, especially because I was early.

I got out and headed over to her. She hopped out all smiles. I just shook my head.

"Well, hello to you too."

"What's up? Pop the hood."
She rolled her eyes and went to do as I said. This time, I had my reader to tell me what the issue was. And as I predicted, her damn engine about to go.
"It's definitely ya engine."
"Oh my fucking gawd, man."
"I told you I had a spot we could go and get another one that's rebuilt. It doesn't cost that much as a brand new one would."
I was trying to give her the best deal. I wouldn't want her to take it to a dealership and have them charge her an arm, leg, some ass, and a foot.
"Okay, can we go today? Like can you start it today?"
I glanced down at my watch checking the time, then back over to her. She seemed desperate. Lucky for her, I was done with everything for the day. I waved her on to get in the car with me. The radio was playing low, and she reached over and turned my shit up. I hit the brakes so hard she jerked forward catching the dashboard.
"What the fuck!"
"Aye, yo, listen. When you in someone else shit, you don't touch nothing. That's straight disrespectful."
She sucked her teeth and crossed her arms.
"Ya ass is rude as fuck. It's irking."
I smirked and turned my shit back at the level I had it. I like listening to music, but I be in deep thought most of the time, and just a lil background melody is all I needed. I didn't go around with my system at full blast. That's what attention seekers do. I don't need attention.
"Wait here."

Her getting out the car was pointless. I knew the guy, and I sent him a text saying I was on my way and what I was coming to get. Once I paid him, he had his men bring the engine out and stick it in my trunk.

"How much was it?"

"Chill, just relax."

There she goes again, rolling her eyes and sucking her teeth.

"Something in ya tooth?" I asked curiously.

"No! I'm just tired of ya mouth."

"If you haven't noticed by now, I just don't give a fuck, take it or leave it."

With that said, she shut the hell up and let me do me. The whole time I was working, she was on her phone either texting or calling. But the way her shit kept ringing, I was about to think her ass sold work. By the time I was done, it was dark, and I was tired, hungry, and in need of another shower.

"Can I at least get you something to eat?"

With everything I did, I only charged her 500, which basically was the engine. Now since she was offering food, I'll take that too. I followed her to this spot that you can smell the shit from the parking lot.

I surveyed the area. Rashidah was standing by the door waiting for me. I felt dirty and not in the mood to sit down and eat. But I wasn't inviting her ass to my crib, and I damn sure wasn't going to hers, so I had no choice but to sit there with her.

"I want to thank you again for hooking me up. I thought I was going to be dishing out at least 1200. Shiid, now I can go shopping."

Women, they always want to go shopping when they have a few extra dollars instead of saving the shit. And half the time they don't even need new stuff, they just want it.

"You would do better by saving the extra money."

"What?"

"I'm sitting across from you, so I know you heard what I said. What is the point in spending money that originally was going to something purposely, but now on material things."

She stopped eating and looked at me to see if I was serious. I schooled her a lil on how shit is and how it should be, but what the holdup is between the two. If you don't have a steady income that's flowing, then why go ham? That's living for the people. Mafuckas go wrong. Look at me, I walk around looking typical and can easily be judged, but that's okay. I want mafuckas to think whatever they want. She wasn't that bad after all. I stayed longer than I intended to, and she ate that shit up.

Chapter 21

Jequell

It was cold as shit outside this morning, had a nigga balls feeling chilly. Shy had my ass up early taking her shopping. I started to tell her hell, but I promised her we would go. I don't know why females think shopping means start early in the morning and be out all day. This was one of the main things I hate when we're in stores. She wanted everything and had to try everything on.

This nut ass dressing room was packed, and I felt like a whole nut sitting there. Some pretty bitch walked out of one and stopped in the full-length mirror, looking at herself in a dress she had on. I watched her in awe. She wasn't definitely a bad one, crim. I guess after deciding she was going to get it, she noticed me looking at her and winked.

A small smile formed as I made sure Shyanne wasn't coming out. I motioned to her and asked where her phone was. She looked confused at first but then went to get it. I hurriedly put my number in it and whispered for her to call me. She nodded and went on back in just as Shy was stepping out.

"Come on, bae. I want all of these." She handed me a pile of clothes, and I just took the shit to the counter to pay.

Lil momma stood in line behind us, unbothered. I knew I was gon' like her ass.

Me up there with Shy ain't bother her ass not one bit. As I grabbed the bags and walked past, I blew her a kiss. She laughed and shook her head. A few hours later, we had burned the stores down. I spent seven racks on a bunch of bullshit if you asked me. But Shy was happy, and when she whipped my dick out in the car, I knew it was fixing to be a long night.

*****

I climbed out of bed the next day and went to my mom's. She was in the living room looking at something on the TV.

"What's up, heifer?"

"Oh, I got ya heifer, lil nigga. The hell you want anyway? Shyanne must have kicked you out."

"Wrong! She still sleeping and dreaming about the way I stretched her walls last night," I told her with a smile.

"I don't wanna hear about ya lil dick. Get on somewhere. Come in here with ya bullshit," she rambled off as I got up laughing.

She shouldn't have tried to play me, talking about I got kicked out. I pay the majority of the rent. Even if she wanted to she couldn't put me out. Ask her how the last time went when she changed the locks.

I got a text from an odd number. My flags went straight up until I read it, and it was lil momma from the mall. I went into my room, locked the door, and hit the camera button to call her.

"Hey, you."

"What's up, girl? What you up to?"

"Nothing, I was chilling and thought about you giving me ya number."

"Yeah, you were hurting my eyes, so I had to pursue you."

She fell out laughing, and I couldn't help but geek myself. All morning I was on the phone with this girl. She was a lil bit older than me, but what does age have to do with it? I was digging her pretty ass. Had a nigga setting up a time and place to meet. Now I just had to figure out how I was gon' get away from Shy later. We planned to go out for dinner, and I could still take her, but the only issue was afterwards. How the hell was I supposed to get away after? Once I came up with a plan, I rolled over and got me some more sleep. It was going to be a long night, but I was up for it, though.

My ma had her music on max and woke me up. Even though I was sick about that, I was glad I did get up. There were a few missed calls from Shy and texts cussing me out for not picking up. I brushed my teeth and wiped the coal out my eye before calling her back.

"What's up, baby?"

"Don't fucking 'what's up baby,' me. Where the fuck you go this morning, and why you leave without waking me up first? You see the shit you do?"

I sighed and shook my head. This girl will find the smallest things to clown about. I could leave the toothpaste open in the bathroom, and she would go ape shit.

"I came to my mom's, Shy, damn. And I just woke up."

"Uhm mmm. Nigga let me find out. What time you coming, so I know to be dressed?"

"Give me an hour."

I hung up from her and hopped my dirty dick in the shower. I stayed in there an extra 10 minutes just to make sure I washed my balls squeaky clean. I found some fits to throw on, and I had just enough time to slide over to Akeem's crib to get a cut. I sent him a text, and he said he was there.

Bro was a beast with the clippers. Nigga always had us on some shitty fresh. I smoked while he did his thing. He gave me a few lines for a design in my shit. I peeled off $40, but he ain't want it. I stay trying to give him money, but he always says when it comes to us, he's good. I respect that, but it still didn't stop me from trying to give it to him. That was just natural with me.

Shy must have seen me coming because soon as I hit her crib, she came right out the door. She looked real good, but I ain't wanna start no shit with her. We would never make it out anywhere.

"Hey, baby booski."

"You always saying some extra shit. The hell is a baby booski?"

She giggled and shrugged. We made our way to La'cinta's. I didn't come as often as my brother did, but I loved the atmosphere. I never felt like I had to hold a strap there, but it was around. We placed our order and started talking, but the conversation went a whole other way when she got to talking about us and how long she had to wait for me.

"Real shit, crim, the fuck is so wrong with what we got already?"

"As far as what we have, nothing. I just know that at any given time you can go out and be with another woman, and I can't technically say anything."

I took a deep breath, getting aggravated. She was blowing my shit.

"When was the last time you had to come to me about another bitch? Huh? Like, you sure know how to fuck up a night, yo."

"Baby, I'm not trying to fuck up the night, but what are we doing if we can't sit here and have a normal conversation about us? And just because I haven't had to say shit to you about another bitch don't mean you ain't fucking with one."

I already knew what she was trying to do. She wanted me to trip myself up and say I'm fucking around. But on the hood, I had been chilling since she got in her feelings the last time. And seeing ol' girl was the first time since then that I kind of entertained somebody.

I stopped talking, and she knew what time it was. Since she fucked the mood up, I didn't even have to do my lil thing to get away from her ass. When we finished, I took her home. She tried to put up a lil fuss about me not coming in, but I told her to shut my fucking door and move. She shut it alright, she damn near broke my shit from slamming it too hard. I started to get out, but the time wasn't on my side, and I was almost late.

"I was starting to think you stood me up."

"Oh naw, I just had to tie up some loose ends."

We grabbed a table and ordered drinks. I had her laughing the whole time. It was good to actually be chilling and not getting cussed out for the small, stupid shit. We most definitely could do this shit again.

Chapter 22

Rashidah

I was on my way to finesse me a nigga when my car started making a weird ass noise. At first, I thought maybe I ran over something, but then it kept doing it. I just pulled over and popped the hood, knowing damn well I didn't know anything about what I was doing or what I was looking at. I was just about to call triple A when Akeem came and asked what was the problem. It was such a blessing to see his face and for him to help me. I thought the nigga was on some goofy time when he pulled off in my shit. Soon as he hit the corner coming back, I calmed down. It's crazy that this happened to my car, but it was fate for it to be him who helped me out. I felt like I was in there when he said bring it by over the weekend.

His smart, rude, pretty ass mouth irked me when he wouldn't give me his number, though. I had actually looked forward to that. When I say I was counting the hours down to the day when it was time, I got up early just to see what I was putting on. The day I saw him, I went to check out the location. It wasn't much to see, I just had to know where he was taking me.

I showed up earlier than he did, and I don't think he liked that because when he noticed I was there, his facial expression changed a bit. Only if he knew I was from the streets, and I moved like a nigga. I played it off like I was really distraught that it was my engine. Whatever it was and whatever it cost, I didn't care. As long as it was fixable.

This fucker almost made me hit my fucking head on his dash trying to be spiteful over a nut ass radio. I sat back and was quiet the rest of the way, fearing that I would say or do something that could potentially fuck all this up. I was getting somewhere, and any lil thing would ruin it. Wasn't every day I would be riding shot gun with Akeem.

I hated to admit it, but because of the hard time he had given me, I slept with this nigga walking around in my dreams. The whole time he did his thing, I kept stealing glances and looks at him. His got damn body was so tight it made me look down at myself and wonder if I should hit the gym and do a couple crunches and squats.

He finished, and I didn't want it to end, so I invited him out to eat and prayed he wouldn't turn me down. I almost jumped out my damn skin when he said yeah. The only place that came to mind was Cecily's. Their food was to die for. It was cooked with soo much love. I was in awe of this nigga. He spoke with so much confidence and knowledge of what he was talking about.

Like the sponge that I am, I soaked it right up. Once he got to talking, I shut. If this was going to keep him with me, then bitch I was a mime. I could tell he was very passionate about making money and saving it. That showed, and I□ knew he had it, which was my sole purpose of getting close to his ass. He had something I wanted, and if it killed me, I was going to get it.

Chapter 23

Hasan

I went to check on something, and soon as I got what I came for, Nia was calling and saying she was ready. I ain't have a real destination in mind, I just wanted the company. Her company. We went and did our thing for the rest of the day then grabbed a room. It was money well spent because this bitch was nice as shit. I took my gun off my hip and placed it on the dresser close to me.

I choked off the loud when she did the same. I think I just fell in love. This lil bitch was gangsta. It was safe to say she matches my fly. Although, that one is in clear view, the one on my ankle was still attached and easy to access. Now that I knew she be packing too, I had to really watch her ass closely.

She got on her knees behind me on the bed and started working her hands into my back and shoulders.

Damn, that shit felt good. I almost let my guard down until she moved. My senses came back, and I pulled her from behind me into my lap. She could have easily slit my throat or popped one in me.

"Relax, Hasan. You made me come with you, remember?"

"Lil girl, I ain't make you do shit. You really wanted to come, that's why you ain't put up a fuss. Stop that bullshit, yo."

"Maybe I did, but you always got to be so uptight. You make me nervous acting like that. Shiid, is there something I should know or be on edge about?" I looked at her and grabbed her long hair. Not rough, but tight. "Naw, that's just my character, Nia. And if you can't get down with that then I can get the fuck on, crim."

She yanked her hair back and got in my face.

"First of all, don't you ever pull on my hair like that again unless you behind me. And second, I never said I couldn't get with shit. I just asked is there something I should be worried about. As you can see, I ain't never scared, and if a nigga was to come through that door right now gunning for you, I'd buss back," she gritted.

My dick instantly rocked up under her.

That heavy shit she just talked had me wanting to fold her ass into a pretzel. And the way she said it, I knew her ass wasn't lying about bussing. But would it really be for me? Or to save her own life? Either way, it wouldn't matter 'cause ain't a soul coming through that door or anywhere for that matter gunning for me. I flipped her lil ass over and climbed on top of her, resting my hand around her neck.

She reached up and pulled my shirt over my head, gliding her fingers down the wash board. I might not work out like Akeem, but a nigga was till cut up naturally. We both got caught up in the moment. She took my lip into her mouth and tugged on it. I wasn't a kisser because I barely liked bitches, but lil momma can have that.

With my hand still around her neck, I used my other one to lift up her shirt and bra. They jumped out like a swat team ready to run down on something. Using my teeth, I pulled on them, and her breathing got heavy. I knew I was starting to drive her ass crazy cause she was digging her nails into my back. Next, I pulled her joggers off. She ain't have any panties on. Lil freak bitch.

I was impressed by what I saw, but that was my business, and I didn't care to share it with her ass. She reached up and wrapped her arms around my neck. Both my hands went under her ass as I picked her up to sit on my lap. The way her tongue slithered through my mouth, I was getting harder by the slob. The heat was just radiating from her pussy. I could smell her sex, and it was definitely sweet.

Done playing games with her ass, I reached into my pants and got a condom out. She took it from my hand, opened with her mouth, and put it on the same way. Her mouth formed into a 'O' while she ate my shit up like a corn on the cob. The shit that was coming out my mouth was unheard of. I started to get ashamed and almost grabbed at my ankle gun to give her ass an arm warmer.

She climbed up my body and flopped down on my dick.

"Ahhh," we both let out.

The gushy shit she had was lethal. I would truly have to put a GPS on this bitch if I took her serious. She moved her hips in a way only an island girl can do. Drums started going off in my head, and I was losing control along with concentration. I grabbed on to her hips and plowed my dick in her.

"Whooooaaa, Iyyy poppie," she moaned all sexily and shit.

Her head fell back, leaving her neck exposed, and I started sucking on her shit. It kept me from moaning my damn self. With my knees in a squat position, I started to wash machine her gooiness. She really was scratching my back up, and I almost dropped her ass. I couldn't hold it in any longer. No matter how many times I pulled out to calm down the moment, I put it back in, her shit suctioned me up.

"Arrrrggh," I growled.

"Faster, Hasan."

With a quick four strokes, I fell back on the bed with her still on top of me. Nia rolled over and went into the bathroom. While she was in there, I got the strength to get up and look at her hammer to see if it was really loaded. And hell yeah, that mafucka was, full clip. If this pretty face nice ass chick walking around strapped with big shit, then I need to do some homework on her ass. That shit doesn't seem right.

"You ready to take me back to my car?"

I looked over at her standing in the doorway, naked. Her body was so tight, I lowkey wanted to go another round, but she had other plans. I just got up and put the rest of my stuff back on. She crossed the room doing the same. We ain't say too many words to each other the whole ride back to her wheel.

Nia leaned over and kiss me then got out, still not saying anything. I ain't know what to get from this or take from it, so I said fuck it. If she was gon' act dumb like a child, then that's what it is. I didn't even wait until she was in her car good before I got up out of there. Akeem's crib was my destination. I needed him to do some background patrolling.

Chapter 24

Travis

Work was popping today. All the homies were there, and we clowned all shift from clock in to clock out. Now now we were at happy hour throwing hella drinks back.

"Aye, Trav, look at this bitch. Her ass can't possibly be real."

I scanned lil momma from head to toe, and yes, her shit was phat. "I don't know, crim, you see the cuff at the bottom? Only a real ass can have that, on the hood."

"Naw man, her shit is fake."

They started really clowning on her, but I was gon' do them one better. I walked over to shawty and stood facing her side.

"Listen, right. My squad believes that ya ass isn't real. Me being an ass man declared it is. Care to prove any of us wrong?"

She giggled then turned around and walked over to where we all were sitting. "For the record, niggas, this is what I was born with. Can't no plastic surgeon make this shit look this good." She twirled with a wink as she came back over to me.

They fell out laughing and talking shit.

"I'm Camille, and you are?"

I took her hand and placed a kiss on it. "Travis."

We chopped it for a cool minute, just getting to know the basics about each other, and I didn't leave out the part that I have a woman. She was cool with that, actually told me to treat her right. We did exchange numbers before I took my drunk ass home.

In the middle of the night, Emana woke up and couldn't breathe because her nose was stopped up. I reluctantly climbed my big ass out of bed and left to go to the store for something to help her ass. Some niggas were in the store loud as shit at 3:00 in the morning. I ignored them and got what she needed then went to pay for it.

I couldn't get to my car before one of them came running up on me asking where the bread at. I cussed myself for not having my strap on me. I was so busy trying to get this girl her stuff that it didn't dawn on me to grab it before I left. I really ain't have but 200 on me. Now I was pissed that I had that. But I wasn't a hoe nigga, and he was gon' go through hell before I gave it up.

"Nigga, what money? I should be asking you where the fucking money at, crim." I stepped in his face.

This bitch ass nigga wasn't expecting for me to boss up on his ass. Must have had it in his head that I was a nut and would have given him whatever he wanted because he was waving a gun around in my face.

I started to laugh as I stepped even closer. If it was my time to go tonight, then so be it. It is what it is. He backed up some, but not before I snatched his piece and shot his ass in the stomach. Bitch nigga got me all way fucked up if he thought this shit was sweet. His mans came running out, and I didn't give him a chance to draw. I lit his ass up too. Amateur ass fuck boys. It was nobody around, but I wasn't taking any chances, so I went back in the store and told the clerk to give me the tapes.

He handed them over with no problem, and I dipped. I was mad as fuck that I caught two bodies in the middle of the night. Them niggas lucky they already got it because once I tell my brother's what happened, they probably would want to come back and kill them all over again for the fuck of it. We ride for one another. When I got to the crib, I threw the bag to Emana, and she looked at me like I lost my mind, but fuck it. I could have gotten killed tonight on some random pick up bullshit for medicine.

A nigga wasn't even sleepy anymore. I rolled up and sat in the living room with all the lights out, chiefing to myself. Since I wasn't sure what niggas had going on, I sent out a text saying link up in the morning or some time later. It was no surprise that Hasan's crazy ass was up and wanted to know if I was straight. I chuckled and told him yeah. Now that I was home good and high, I was cool.

Mana came out and turned on all the lights.

I got pissed off again.

"Fuck is you doing man?"

"You better stop cussing at me, and what the fuck is the problem? You weren't doing all this when you left out to go to the store"

I took a deep breath and got up to walk past her, but she pulled my arm, stopping me in my tracks.

"Yo chill, you killing my mood even more. I don't want to talk about it right now."

She just let go with a sad face and went back into the room. I kind of felt bad for treating her like that, but she knew when I wasn't in the mood, and when I'm like that to leave me the fuck alone.

I tried to get some sleep, and when it was getting good, my phone started going off all crazy from all my brothers. These niggas would all get up at the same time and hit me. Grumbling, I sat at the end of the bed and answered Jequell since he was the one calling when I picked up the phone.

"Yo, crim, what's the science?"

"Man, listen, you know my words can't travel through this phone I'll be at Ma's crib in an hour."

"Bet that."

I told the same thing to the rest of them.

Mana was gone by the time I got up, and I knew I had some making up to do. That was light, though. It didn't take much to make her mad, and it was the same way to making her happy. She never asked for much but my honesty, love, and time.

Ma was just pulling off when I pulled up. She honked the horn and asked was I okay. Nodding my head yes to her, and she hollered that she left food on the table but to clean her kitchen back up when we were done eating. I was starving too. I loved that woman. I slapped hands with everybody then made myself a plate. These niggas were already two in by the I made mine.

I ran everything down to them, and they were on my ass about not being strapped. Said even if I had to run out to the car for something, I better have that bitch tucked under my nuts. Never go anywhere without it. And I know that. Shiid, I lived by that, but I was caught slipping that night. We got to talking about females and a whole bunch of bullshit, which made me think of Camille. I hadn't talked to her.

Soon as I sent the text, she texted back quickly. We went back and forth for an hour. She was really cool people. The conversation was a friendly one but interesting. Since I had off, I kicked my feet up and chilled right at my ma's crib.

Chapter 25

Nia

It had been days since the last time I had talked to Hasan. The way he fucked me, I had to reevaluate myself. I didn't want to admit that I had met my match, and I still won't admit it. That's why I think I should just stay away and tell Rashidah to pull me out. They all were in their usual spots when I walked in. All engrossed in their phones with devious smiles on their faces.

"Uh, hello!"

"What you hollering for?" Simone sassed.

I rolled my eyes at her and took a seat. They went right back to their phones, and I was starting to think that it was not business on the other end. Here I was about to break it off with a mark, and they were all in there cheesing. Ain't no bitch got them breaking their face. I shook my head and got up to leave the house.

I didn't have a destination, and I was bored. Really didn't want to bother him, but he was my last resort at this moment.

"Yo," he barked.

I kind of missed his ignorant ass

"What's up, nigga?"

"Ain't shit, Nia. Let me hit you back, I'm dealing with something right now."

"Naw, you ain't got to." I hung up feeling played.

This clown just rushed me off the phone like I was a nobody. I don't do well with that type of shit. Then he sent a text and told me to get out my feelings. He was really busy but wanted to see me in a bit. The smile that crossed my face was one I couldn't control.

Since I had nothing to do until he called me back, I went to visit my mother. She was always a good time when I had nothing to do. She was pulling trash cans in when I go there. I hopped out and helped her with the rest.

"Ma, it's only you here. Why do you have so much trash?"

"I don't know, Nia, I just do," she fussed.

I could see now that she wasn't in a good mood. Some days it was like that for her, especially when she starts thinking about our Dad.

"Ma, you okay?" I stopped and grabbed both her hands, making her look at me. I could tell she had been crying because of the bags that formed under her eyes.

"Chica, I just miss your father so much. I feel lonely here sometimes. You guys do come and visit, but it's not enough."

I could understand where she was coming from.

"What can I do—no, what can we do to fix it, Momma?"

Her face lit up, and she wiped at the tears that started flowing again.

"Have a baby."

My face frowned upon hearing her say that. She knew damn well what we believed, and that having a baby was out.

"Now, Ma, you already know what the deal is with that."

She snatched her hands away from me and went into the house. I took a minute before I went in after her. "Y'all make me sick with all these damn rules and shit. Is life really that serious? I know we hit a few rough patches, but don't you ladies think it's time to start living again? You will never excel holding on to hurt, chica. Never."

Her words went deep. I thought about everything she said and went back to me wanting to be outside of this shit sometimes. But when this is all you know, what else is there to do?

Hasan had hit me and said to fall through. I gave my ma a big hug and kiss, telling her to get some rest before I left her. Her words just kept playing over in my head as I went to the spot where he was. He stood in the door all tall and chocolate, making me like his ass, knowing I shouldn't.

"What's up, girl?"

He one arm hugged me and locked up. The place looked a little different from the last time we were there. Homelier. Maybe he does stay there after all. I took my shoes off and tucked my feet under me. He took the spot next me and pulled my hair.

"What is up with you doing that?"

He shrugged and just looked at me. I started to get uneasy like maybe he knew what my sisters and I were up to. Then he spoke up,

"Why you carry around heat?"

That was definitely not what I expected to come out his mouth. But I gave the best answer I could give without giving too much.

"Because we live in a gang infested city where anybody is liable to get ran down on. And just because I have a pretty face doesn't mean I'm exempt."

I stretched the truth a lil bit, but what I said was true. At any given moment, I could be the chosen one. And if that ever was the case, I'd always be ready.

I guess my answer was good enough because he dropped the hard stare and got a little more comfortable. He hadn't been this relaxed either time I was around like he was today. I thought maybe I was getting somewhere. But could I really think like that? Lately, I found myself with this nigga on my brain all the time now. And not in a malicious way, but sexual. He reached out and pulled me over to him, and I laid my head in his lap.

He turned some movie on called *Snow from the Bluff*, and it was good. I was so into it that I was hollering at the TV. We fell out laughing at my ass. My nipples got hard from it being cold in there, so he went and got me a throw blanket. I tried fighting my sleep again, but I couldn't. I felt at peace. Something my crazy ass hadn't felt in years.

I woke up in a bed this time and next to him. Of course, Hasan wasn't completely asleep. Soon as I opened my eyes and moved, he did too. I don't think I could get anything past his ass. And I had better be careful because if he even thinks I'm on some nut ball shit, I'm done.

Chapter 26

Jequell

I was sitting across the table from lil momma. She was all smiles and shit, had a nigga feeling goofy sitting there breaking my face. But I couldn't deny the attraction I had toward her. This was our fourth date, and I still hadn't hit that. I wasn't tripping off that, though. Shy ass takes all the nut to where I wouldn't have shit left to give the next.

"Jequell, you silly as hell, man." The way my name rolled off her tongue made me second guess not hitting that.

My neck jerked with a sting so bad, I immediately went for my gun.

"Bitch, you got to be kidding me right now!" Shy stood there with her hands on her hips, ready for war.

"What the fuck I tell you about putting ya hands on me, Shyanne?"

"Bitch, fuck you! You can tell me to wait on you, yet you out here entertaining some bitch!" She went to reach for the knife and tried to cut me.

I jumped back right on time.

The whole damn restaurant was now up out their seats watching and waiting. Looking on at us, well me, to see what I was going to do next. I felt like soon as I lift a hand they would be on the phone with the rollers. I gave her the death stare and moved around her with Simone in tow. I peeped her grill Shyanne as she passed by.

That was the last time she was going to embarrass me like that. The girl was out of control. I know I probably hurt her by telling her to wait for me then see me out with somebody, but she still did too much. Simone sat in the front seat of my car laughing. I didn't think nothing was funny, but to her it was hilarious.

"Yo, why you keep laughing? Let me smack you in the neck and then try and cut you."

"You can try, and I'll have to shoot ya ass."

"Shoot me? What you know about shooting?"

"Oh, I know a thing or two, baby."

I smirked at her and kept driving. My phone was going off so bad, and I knew it was Shyanne that was calling. I just turned it off. As of right now, we were through. I just couldn't be who she wanted me to be. And tonight made me realize that I couldn't hold her up because of it.

The next morning, I woke up to the rollers banging on my mom's door. She cussed them out and they put her in cuffs. Now I was spazzing, but that ain't do nothing but land me an ass whooping by them. They beat me the fuck up with the cuffs on, bussing my nose. I was sick, and envisioned killing every last one of them slow. I even offered them to take the cuffs off and let's go toe to toe. Those pussies read me my rights and said I was under arrest for a homicide.

I had caught so many bodies that I wish I knew which one they were referring to. But with blood dripping from my nose, I held my head up as they shifted me off. I thought they were really going to lock my ma up too, but as soon as I was put in the back of the cop car, they let her go. She mouthed to me that she got me. I winked at her and sat back, trying to get comfortable. Those cuffs were so tight, one wrong move and my hands were going to fall off.

After hours of questioning, they finally took me to a holding cell. The bastards ain't even give me my phone call. I wasn't worried about that, though; I knew Ma' was on everything handling her business. A whole few days went by before they sent me off to the county. At that point, all I wanted was a shower and a cot to sleep on. A nigga was funky and tired.

I thought about Shyanne, our fall out, then about Simone and the lil time we spent. My brothers and the work we put in. Everything was running through my mind like a marathon playing back to back. I wasn't sure how long I was gon' be there or what kind of evidence they had on a nigga. However, it didn't matter. I wasn't a snitch, nor was I gon implicate myself. I will plead the fifth!

Chapter 27

Simone

I hadn't told my sisters about me dealing with Jequell, and I wasn't going to say shit either. I was tired of being caught up in this bullshit, but not have a real regular life outside of it. I was doing my own thing out shopping when I saw him. I thought he was real cute, but I figured he was with somebody being as though he was sitting outside a women's dressing room. I kept on with my business. But his eyes never left my body, and I naturally winked at him. This bold ass fool wanted my number.

Once we exchanged our math and went on a few dates, I was ready to see what that was about. He wore sweat pants on one occasion, and I damn near bussed it wide open for his ass on sight. Now, the lil stunt his lil bitch pulled was funny as hell. Her nerd ass was really going to cut him right there in a public setting where everybody was watching. I was glad he didn't react the way she probably wanted him to.

Here it is 7:00 at night, and I done called him at least five times. Still haven't got any answer, and I started to get mad as fuck. Just when I picked up the phone to send him a reckless ass text, his number was calling me back.

"Oh, these the type of games you play, Jequell?"

"This is Jequell's mother, and who are you?"

The way she asked that almost made me get busy with her ass too, but then I thought about my own mother and what I would do if a mafucka mouth got flip with her.

"Hello, I'm Simone. Is Jequell around?"

"No, Simone, he isn't. I'm only about to tell you this so you don't keep calling him back to back. He got locked up this morning, and when I hear from him, I will let him know you have been calling him, okay?"

I swallowed the lump that formed in my throat and told her okay.

I would be lying if I said, oh well, to the shit she just told me because it kind of put a damper on my mood. I had just started to feel alive again with the lil dates we would go on, and now all that shit had come to a complete stop. Ever since my ex was killed a few years ago, I hadn't really done much but set these niggas up. Although the outcome was worth it, our lives go right back to boring. Back then, I thought I was in love and had found the one man who truly had my heart, but my heart was just something that pumped in my chest to him. The shit he did to me had me so fucked up in the head and super cool on men, which made it easier for me to put in that work. He used to have me clean, scrub, then lick his feet when he would get mad. Suck his dick right after he blatantly fucked another bitch in front of me.

He would tie me up and make me watch him have sex with multiple women, and when he was done, I would have to wash him from head to toe. He even had me eating his ass a few times. Honey, I done been through it all. A whole doormat for four years. Get this, though. Out of the blue, he was killed. Don't know how it happened, and didn't try to find out. His mom and them said they think I had something to do with it. Shiid, I wish I had something to do with it.

There is no way they didn't know how he treated me all those years, and all they did was turn a blind eye to the bullshit. But I couldn't really expect them to say or do anything. They were scared of his ass as well, and I never liked any of them. When they came around, I stayed to myself, and I only spoke when I was in a good mood. To them, it appeared that we were so happy and working on marriage.

Yeah, this clown made me wear an engagement ring out in public. I was his property. When Ra brought the idea to me, I was spiteful, on some revenge shit toward all men who was fuck niggas. My first kill was unplanned, but I felt damn good afterward and knew I was going to do it again. See, we aren't supposed to kill our marks. We set them up and rob them, but sometimes you can't stop shit from happening. Ra be pissed too.

Anyway, since I didn't have that nice distraction around anymore, I called up my victim and told him I'll be through. He had big bucks but was stingy as fuck. I couldn't wait to have his ass on his knees begging. He was making me work too damn hard.

Chapter 28

Akeem

I was sick that my lil brother was sitting out the county on murder charges. That was a low blow. I always instilled in them to be careful, but his ass along with Hasan are hardheaded. I was on my way to this lawyer to drop bread on him to represent Quell on the case. The mafucka was charging me up too. I told him for this price, he had better get his ass out scott free. This was a small set back, and not money wise because that wasn't the issue. Just him being in there and not out here with the rest of us.

"So, what now, Akeem? He still hasn't called yet?"

"Ma, you got to relax. Being all anxious and dramatic isn't gon' help the man get out. We just have to sit back and wait, that's all. Ain't like you haven't been through this before with me."

I looked at the clock and saw the time. Once I dropped my mom off, I met up with Rashidah. She had been keeping my interest a lil. But real shit, she is unpredictable, and I'm keeping her close so I can figure out her whole thing.

They say keep ya friends close and enemies closer. She was sitting down, but I could see her ass just spread all over that damn chair. From the lil hints she'd been throwing, I knew she wanted me to jump her bones. I had just been holding off on blessing her with good dick. She the type who would cling because she already tryna do it now.

"What's up, Ra?"

Nothing but smiles. She got up to hug me. I swear, she liked to just touch my black ass.

"Hey, what happened? Why you cancel yesterday?"

"Had some important shit to handle."

"Everything alright? Can I help?"

"Naw, you good."

"So, since I turned you on to a recipe, let me actually make one for you."

I thought about that and didn't mind a cooked meal that I will watch her prepare. She might try and stick some shit in it to kill me.

"Cool, where would you like to do this at and when?"

"Your place and now."

"Naw."

I wasn't in the mood to laugh at her. She acted surprised that I said no.

"Okay, then, we can go to my spot."

We first made a pit stop at the market to get the shit she wanted to cook and then to this lil nice spot out of sight of everything, but still local. I walked past there a few times when I was on a nightly stroll. When I walked in, all my alarms went off, and I immediately knew she didn't live there. It didn't have that woman's touch to it. Shit kind of felt new.

Instead of asking questions, I watched her closely the rest of the night. The food was on point, as I expected. Baby girl can burn, no doubt.

"How is it?"

"It's good, where the bathroom at?"

She pointed to a door that was slightly opened. Bathroom had nothing in it, not even a damn rug, a mat, or a curtain. The shower looked like it hadn't even been touched. It had that new smell to it. Even the toilet was brand new. There was nothing in the cabinets, no feminine toiletries under the sink. Whose place was this really?

When I came out the bathroom, she was doing something on her phone. Mine started to ring itself with my momma calling. I got back up and walked outside on the lil balcony.

"Yeah, mom?"

"Bro," I heard Jequell's voice, causing me to smirk.

"What's popping, nigga?"

"Aww, man, ain't shit. You know how this shit go."

"Already."

We chopped it up for the remainder of the ten minutes. Couldn't say too much over the phone, but I told him I would be up to see him in a few days. He let me know that Has and Trav put money on his books, so he was straight for a while.

"Akeem, are you okay?"

I turned around to see Rashidah standing in the sliding door. I nodded at her and gestured for her to give me a minute. I ain't need her all up in my conversation eavesdropping. I wrapped up my call and went back inside. By now the music was playing in the background, and she was trying to set the mood.

Coming to sit next to me, Ra popped open some wine. She acted like she knew me or something. I don't drink, but I will indulge in some wine, Riesling at that. Classical thug is what you can call me. But, before I got to sipping anything with this broad, I needed to know a few things.

"How long you been here?" I asked, referring to this crib.

"A couple months, why?"

I studied her before I went on with my questioning. Even though she had answered a couple months, I didn't believe her. My silence was making her a lil uncomfortable, and that's what I liked.

"You got something to tell me?"

She shifted in her seat, and I moved closer to her as she backed up.

"Uh no, why you asked me that?" Her mouth turned flip, more defensive.

I could see that I was getting under her skin by asking questions like that. I let it go for now, but I wouldn't forget her reaction. We finished off the whole bottle with her being more lit than I was. I should have been surprised when she got up and pulled her shirt over her head and then made my lap was her next destination.

"You're so handsome and sexy to me," she said, using her fingers to outline my lips.

I grabbed her wrist and moved them. I mean, her hands can appear clean, but you not fixing to be moving them across my lips and shit.

"And mean," she added with a small chuckle.

"I'm not mean. I'm just different from a lot of men."

"Different. Huh? How so?"

I didn't come there to explain shit to her. She had been wanting this dick and made me that food. She just earned herself a lil taste. I stood up with her still in my lap and carried her thick ass to the back. She told me which room to go in, and I dropped her ass down on the bed. A bed that looked untouched also.

This here wasn't a take ya time thing. I pulled my dick out my pants, but left them on just stroking it. Ra's mouth hit the bed frame at the size and girth. I was only semi hard. She was gon have to do a trick or two to see it grow to its full potential. Collecting herself, she got on her knees and removed the rest of everything she had on. Her body was tight in all the right places, and with her clothes off, I got to see it fa' real.

We could still hear the music, which she used to do a lil sexy dance for me. I was half impressed, though. At this point, I just wanted to fuck and dip off on her. Tired of the lil show she tried to put on, I snatched her ankles, pulled her all the way down the bed, and folded them to her neck. Her shit was exposed, and I could see the wetness it carried.

With the tip of my dick, I moved it up and down her clit, causing major friction. She squirmed under me like I was really doing something. I hoped she could take dick. If she couldn't, that would be a disappointment. She looked like she had enough of my playing. I stuck my dick so far in her, she yelled out loud as hell, almost causing a nigga to go deaf.

"What you screaming for? This what you wanted, right?"

Ra couldn't even talk. She was panting like she was having a baby. I Riverfront rambled that pussy. It squirted, creamed, farted and all. My eyes ended up traveling to the closet, and it was empty. That made me damn near go soft. She lied to me. And I don't like liars. The way I started to murder her shit, I had to hurry up because her neighbors probably called the cops already the way she was carrying on.

On some disrespectful shit, I pulled out and bussed all over her neck and face. I was tripping for raw dogging this bitch knowing I lowkey barely liked her ass. I take my clean, free of STDs dick personal.

"I don't like liars," was all I said as I left her laying right there pissed and shocked about the painting I drew on her face.

Chapter 29

Travis

The back seat of this car had me nauseous as fuck! I couldn't smoke out like I wanted to, fearing they wouldn't let me in to see bro. I was sick. Only thing keeping me straight right now was Camille. She had been texting me since we left his morning. Emana was at work and was working late today. Since I worked a double yesterday, they gave me off today. Akeem decided to slide up on Jequell, and I wasn't going to miss it.

That was bro, and in a situation like this one, support was all he needed.

"Nigga, who the fuck got ya goofy ass back there breaking face and shit? I know it's not Emana's boring ass," Has cracked on me.

I laughed and told him to keep my girl's name out his mouth.

"And just to clarify, my bitch ain't boring. She just ain't wild like the whores you entertain."

I blocked his ass out the rest of the ride there. He was known to get annoying because he was always talking shit.

We pulled up to the jail where the line was long as shit to get in. The whole ride there Akeem was quiet. Not his usual observant quiet, but in deep thought. Like something was on his mind kind of quiet. A few times he glanced back in the rear view at me but then kept his eyes trained on the road.

"Aye, bro, you good?"

"Always, crim," he responded, shutting me out of whatever was bothering him.

I didn't feel no type about it, though. That was just how he was. He would take the whole world on his shoulders just to make sure everybody else was good but would never talk about his own problems. Ma said he had been like that since we were young niggas. I didn't understand it, but with him, it wasn't for me to. Luckily, the line moved kind of fast, and we were in, sitting down, and waiting for him in no time. The room was filled with babies crying, women dressed in anything talking loud or fussing. This was definitely a place I never want to be held inside.

Jequell came through the door smiling and joking with the nigga behind him. We all stood up to give out brotherly hugs to our youngin'. It's all love and respect, ya feel me?

"What's cracking, big homie?" Quell said to Akeem all hype.

I was glad it made bro smile a lil. He had a soft spot for us all, but I think the main one always was Quell since he was the youngest. After bringing it in with Has and myself, we sat down and talked about this jam he was in.

"So, listen right, they tryna bang me for that shamtalkin' bout on the block. But I don't know how they gon do that. Shiid, I wasn't there."

He was speaking in codes, but basically, the noodle nigga that ran up on him outside the crib's body was found, and they trying to pin the murder on him.

"Damn. That's out of pocket. What kind of evidence they have that actually points at you?" Has wanted to know.

"The lawyer dude came up here not too long ago and said it was all circumstantial evidence. They really didn't have shit other than what somebody saying they saw," he responded and looked us all in the eye.

That was the code to find out who was or is involved, and take care of them. Akeem still didn't say too much. He added his input and listened to mostly what we had to say. Before we left, he schooled Quell on a few things. Bro will drop them jewels on you and have ya head spinning like crazy.

Quell said he was straight for the most part, and we ain't have to come back up there and to just make sure we were at his court date. The one thing I can say about my brothers is, when they booked, they bid. All the visits and phones calls to us wasn't really their thing. As long as money is on the books and they got everything they need, they good.

I went to see Camille when I got back. She was out doing nothing when I met up with her. She had the most genuine smile that always caused me to smile back.

"Hey, you, how did it go?"

I was lunching and told her my lil brother was booked, and I was on the way to see him earlier. Now she was asking questions that I wasn't comfortable answering, so I changed the subject. Since we weren't that far from Emana's job, I wanted to get the hell out of there. She insisted we go this place that was in the vicinity. I wasn't tryna spoil it for her, but I knew this was dangerous. Everybody at Mana's job knew who I was and loved her ass too much not to tell her if they saw me.

I couldn't get comfortable, and once Camille actually slowed down, she noticed.

"Uh, are you okay, Travis? You don't look like you want to be here."

"That's 'cause I don't."

"Oh," she said, sounding like I took her best friend away.

I wasn't talking about being around her, it was the spot we were at. I explained that to her, and once she got my drift, we bounced and slid off to a park that had a few things going on. Having sex with her was the furthest thing from my mind. She was just a cool ass chick to talk to.

Chapter 30

Rashidah

My walk was slightly different, and as much as I tried to walk normal, it was clear that something was wrong with my ass. Akeem beat my shit up like I gave him herpes, but I will say it was everything I imagined and then some. I was just worried that we were through when we were just getting started. He said he don't like liars right before he left me lying there with his nut sliding down my face like water.

Now, my last nigga did some fucked up shit to me, but what he did was downright disrespectful. When I do talk to him, I will be sure to tell him about his fucking self.

I walked into the house slowly with my face in my phone, trying to play it off. In all reality, I was just trying to throw them off my posture. I couldn't make it up to my room without Nia's lil ass saying something, which caused me to stop and talk.

"Anything new going on with the Akeem character?"

"Uh, not really. He still keeping me at bay. I'm starting to think he's on to me. I mean, from the shit that he asks and how he looks at me, it's like he doesn't trust shit that comes out my mouth."

I was half lying to them. Akeem really does have a way of looking at you like he searching for ya soul. And when he asked me how long had I been there at that apartment, I said a few months, but I had really just grabbed that joint a few weeks ago. I hadn't gotten the chance to make it look like anything. The only reason I got it was because I was trying to stay a few steps ahead of him. I knew he wasn't going to let me come to his crib, but it wasn't a crime that I tried it.

Even my sisters don't know about the spot, and for now, I was going to keep it that way. How I got at this nigga was my business, and my business only. They just needed to be worrying about the assignments they have.

"Well, what's the deal with Hasan?"

"He coming along, I think. I mean, it's still a lot of work to do, but I got this," she answered and got up to walk past me.

I just looked at my other two sisters and climbed the stairs for a much needed bath. The way it hurt for my legs to touch was ridiculous, but I would do it all over again to have a taste of his chocolate ass.

I was gon' give it a few days before I reached out to Akeem. He seemed real bothered when he left, and I needed to play it all back to see what I did, and at what point we went wrong. I thought we were vibing, but the amount of shit I wiped off my face said otherwise.

Chapter 31

Jequell

My ma told me about Simone fucking my phone up the day I got jammed. I had her call her on three ways at first. We chopped it down until the phone time ran out. When I got off with her, I tried my hand at calling Shyanne, but the dizzy bitch changed her number. You know what, though? I wasn't stressing on her ass. Naw, not while I was in here. If they ever let me out, she needed to know that she was gon' have to see me. Our last encounter was bad, but damn. You go and changed ya umber and now you don't know what's going on with me? I guess she don't give a fuck either. I ran with that and pushed her to the back of my head. Today, Simone was bringing her fine ass up there to see a nigga. I hadn't expected her to say she wanted to slide on me, but she was the one who brought it up. And soon as she did, I put the slip in to get her on my visiting list. It took no time, and she took no time falling through. The moment she entered the visiting room, a few niggas, even some who were sitting down with their own women mouthed 'damn'. I sat back and laughed because it damn sure was like that.

She walked that room like it was a runway, and I got more excited with each step she took towards a nigga. "Damn girl, why you coming in here like that? Got these niggas' mouth dripping along with mine."

She giggled, wrapped her arms around my neck, and kissed me with a lil bit of tongue. Umm, I needed that right about now. I got my feels on, cuffing her ass. Her shit always was big and meaty, but today, that shit was on EXTREME. For some reason, I was feeling mushy and talked to her the whole time holding hands. Her shit was so soft compared to my rough ass claws, but Simone ain't mind. She held on with a death grip, keeping a smile on her face the whole time.

"So, what are they saying? Like, is this shit a real live sit down for you?"

"It could be, who knows? But don't worry yaself about that, 'cause I ain't worried. You were free before I came in here, and you still are free to do wateva you want, who eva you want," I informed her.

She looked like she didn't like the sound of what I said, but I was just keeping it a benji. Sitting there really made me think about the selfish shit I did to Shyanne by holding her back from being truly happy because I couldn't commit.

Now, here is Simone acting like she wanted to ride alongside me, but I couldn't have her feeling like she had to. I'm not doing that shit again. Not only did Shy get hurt, I feel a lil broken up too. I had love for the girl, well shit, I still do, but I know I'm no good for her. I like women. Multiple at that. And I'm afraid that one chick is never going to be enough for me.

The guard called my name and told me my time was up. This was the part I hated most. Going back into the jail while everybody else went outside to the free world. I wasn't sweating it, though. My time was coming, and when it does, I'll be good again. Simone got on her tippy toes and grabbed the back of my head, bringing my face close to hers. She attacked my lips like this was the last time she will ever see a nigga. I wasn't going to ask if it was. If that was how she felt, then I had to take that shit on the chin along with everything else I was facing right now. Real niggas do real things.

Chapter 32

Hasan

I was crouched down waiting for this money to show up. Yup, I was back on my grimy shit. Money was slipping away just a lil, and I had to make moves for it to get back and then some. This nigga was eating something, fucking it up to where he didn't even see me creep behind him.

"Open the fucking door," I gritted with my gun jammed in his side.

He froze, dropped his food, and put his hands up. What's up with these clowns getting money but be cold bitch. He opened the door, and I pushed him inside then closed it with my foot.

"Nigga, you know what time it is."

This clown was acting like he ain't know the drill. I moved in close and hit his ass with the butt of my gun, causing blood to ooze from his nose and lip. He put his hands up to stop the bleeding, but it was shooting out like a broken fire hydrant. That also got him moving. He lifted up the deep freezer top and dug all the way to the bottom, pulling out a well packaged block of money.

I knew it was some more around there, but this would have to do for now. I shot him in the thigh, making 'em drop, then fled out the same door, leaving it open. Since I wasn't expecting to be carrying a block of money down the street, I walked with speed over to the jinther. I hit the locks on it as I got closer, then hopped in and got out of there.

This was only two hundred and fifty K. I mean, not much, but it was enough for the day. Bro called me earlier and said he wanted to rap to me about something. Once I got finished counting up and changing, I made my way over. Akeem was sitting down puffing on a cigar. The way that shit smelled, it started fucking with my stomach. I ain't even want to cop a squat.

"I think I may be on to something about them bitches." That had my attention.

"Oh yeah? Why you say that?"

"I got reason to believe, but I'm not sure. It's just a hunch for now. You though, what's the deal with the chick Nia?"

"I mean, ain't shit major. Why? You got some info on her?"

"Naw, I don't, but just pay close attention to her."

"Shiiid, I already do that. Wait, you think she an opp?" He stroked his chin hair. "Could be, I don't know yet." I nodded my head, now way more uneasy about her. Not that I was letting my guard down fully, but she was good company, and her energy matched mine. If she the enemy though, I ain't got no choice but to open her the fuck up for even thinking it was okay to try and get close to a nigga.

"Listen, in the meantime, don't do anything. Keep up with wateva you been doing. Don't make her feel like you not trusting her or giving her a chance."

That's some bullshit, but I trusted his word. He never had me out there looking bad, so it's whatever. I dapped him up and left. My ma had kind of been set tripping since Quell got booked. We all had been checking on her as much as we can. Ain't like we aren't always over there already.

Some pretty chick who resembled somebody I knew, was sitting in the kitchen talking to her when I got there. It felt like I had seen her before, but then, I knew I hadn't because I would have cracked on her.

"Oh, Hasan, hey baby. I want you to meet Simone. This is Jequell's lil friend," she said all happy, but I wasn't the least bit moved.

For starters, how she my bro's friend and I don't know anything about her? Last I checked, he was still checking for Shy's goofy ass. Then she sitting in there all cozy, like how well do my ma know this broad?

"When did Jequell get a new 'friend,' Ma?"

The girl turned her face up but then fixed it when I caught her. My ma rolled her eyes at me and told me to get out her kitchen. What the fuck did I say wrong, though? I thought that was a legitimate question. Since I ain't know lil momma, I sat in the living room eavesdropping on their conversation. They weren't talking about much that I cared for, but I still stayed around and waited until she left.

"You really don't have to be so damn rude all the time, Hasan. Damn. That's a nice young lady, and she seems to really like Quell."

"Ma, I ain't really trying to hear all that. Who the hell is she, and how well do you know her? Quell ain't said shit to us about having a new bitch that he actually liked enough for you to meet her. Then you got her all up in here all welcome and shit."

She waved me off and took a seat, sparking her cigarette. I was really waiting for her to answer me, and when she noticed I was still staring at her, she went off.

"Hasan, I'm a grown ass woman, and who I choose to associate myself with is my mafuckin' business. Y'all niggas ain't holding no weight around here. I happen to like the girl more than that tired ass Shyanne. So, if I wanna bring her into MY home, then so fucking be it!"

I didn't want to hear all that. I got up and told her I was out. If she wanted to have randoms around, fine. But I wouldn't be coming through like that anymore until I knew what was up.

Chapter 33

Nia

Has was taking me to the movies, and I was hype about it. Been a lil minute since I ain't have to be on my shit. He was turning into the perfect man in my eyes. So many times, I wanted to tell Shidah that, but I couldn't do it. Didn't want to hear anyone else say shit about my decision. I had been keeping it to myself. The more time I spent with him, it was becoming clear that setting him up was not in my plans.

I rubbed my body down with the body butter from Bath and Body Works called a Thousand Wishes. It smelled so good, and I just wanted to be Ray J tonight with One Wish. I said fuck panties and let this pussy air out. Since it be cold as hell in the movies, I put on some stretchy pants that made my ass sit out, a Milano Di Rouge sweater, and some knee boots. My hair had the wild look, so I just threw some hoops and a chain on to compliment my fit.

Once I gave myself the once over in the mirror, I winked at the bad bitch staring back and met up with Hasan at his place. I bit my lip when he appeared out the back. He had on a cream color Armani Exchange sweater, black crispy jeans, and black boots. His hair was always cut and freshly spinning. I can say this, I'm glad sis did put me on to him, or else I wouldn't even be getting these opportunities to spend time getting to know the real him or getting wet upon seeing his face.

"What's up, you ready?"

I nodded my head yup, I ain't need to speak. We hopped in his wheel and took off into the night. Fuck tryna hide looking at him, I just couldn't help myself from staring at the man.

And when we left the movie, he put his arm around me, making me feel giddy inside. I told him I was hungry and wanted real food, so we found a lil joint to eat at.

"Yo, what's up with you? Why you been hawking a nigga down all night? Is there something on my face? Talk to me," he said, putting his chicken wing down and licking the hot sauce off his fingers.

I cleared my throat because I was imagining that I was that wing.

"I just can't stop looking at you, that's all. Why? It makes you feel uneasy, Hasan?"

"Somewhat, but long as ain't no bad intentions floating around in ya head while you doing it, we good."

I smirked because it wasn't bad intentions, but it was wild, bad thoughts. I was full by the time we left there and were back at his spot.

I didn't plan to go home, so I got comfy. He watched me strip out of everything and started his way. Since the moment he stepped out the door, I wanted to jump his damn bones. With slow, wet, kisses I made trails all over his body. He was so chocolate and tall with his handsome features, but what grabbed me the most was the gap in his teeth. It's one of a kind and fits him. I didn't know if I was looking for love, but tonight, I was gon' act like it.

I□ unbuckled his pants and let his dick spring to life. It was so meaty and thick, with veins protruding. I□ licked then sucked, spit, slurped, hummed, and gurgled that dick until he had no choice but to relax. I□ told him that tonight it was all his. He was still sitting straight up, so I□ lowered my ass down on his dick and rocked just my hips forward then back. I□ had his ass in a trance because he smacked my ass so hard I□ knew it was gon be a welt there. But, that was just a silent sign. His way of telling me that I□ was working this pussy.

"Shit, Nia!" he mumbled real low.

See, he was the type who didn't want a bitch to do him. He had to be in control, and as far as moaning, that was something he tried to not do. In my case, it would be extremely hard not to. I□ saw this chick do something on a porno, and I□ wanted to try it out. I□ pulled him up and made his back face the wall. I□ took one of my legs and basically went in split mode, standing up with his shoulder holding my leg.

With no hands, I□ put his hard dick back in me and used just my ass to slap against his thigh. He held onto me so tight I□ almost wasn't able to barely move. My shit was slippery wet for Hasan.

"The fuck is you trying to do, man?"

I□ secretly laughed at him bitching, then I□ swung my leg down and danced on the dick.

"Uhmm," we both moaned at the same time.

He stopped me mid twerk and growled as he bussed. I□ wasn't mad. Shiiid, my legs were starting to feel like noodles anyhow.

Chapter 34

Simone

The stare down I got from Hasan had me a bit annoyed. The fuck was his problem anyway? He needed to be worried about Nia, and not me or Jequell. I liked him, and whether he or any of his brothers like me, I will be around. I sat in my car outside of the bitch Shyanne's crib, waiting to see if she pulled up or if she was already home. At this point, if I was all in, there was no way she could have a slight chance with him again. I just don't play that shit. And I know he thinks I probably said fuck it, and would move around, but not at all.

I just didn't want to seem pressed at the moment, so I kind of gave off the impression that what we had was gon' fly. By showing him that I'm a rock no matter what, I got in good with his momma. You know hood niggas love their momma. She was crazy as hell, but I could tell I was gon' get along with her just fine.

The bitch finally walked out her crib. She looked cute or whatever, but of course, I looked way better. Since I wasn't parked that far down, I got out and fixed my clothes. My heels clicked and clacked as I approached her at her car door.

"Excuse you," I said, now standing behind her.

She turned around, flipped her hair, and turned her face up.

"Thought I would pay you a visit and let you know that Jequell is off limits. Don't think about trying to get in contact with him or reaching out to his mother, none of that. Got it?"

She laughed like I was in a comedy show. I stepped closer, getting in her personal space.

"I know you better back the fuck up before we start dancing in a minute. And, as far as Jequell, you can have him and the many visits he can get, sweetie. I'm done and will not be checking on him nor reaching out to anybody. He played with my heart for the last time with yo corny ass, and now he gon' feel my pain sitting in a jail cell. Let him know I said don't drop the soap," she taunted with venom dripping from her voice.

Now, I know I'm not slow, but it sounds to me like she had hands in this.

"Let me get this straight, you know he booked because you put him there?"

"Honey, I didn't put him nowhere. What he in there for is what he did, not me. I just helped out a lil by speeding up the process of finding him." She said that shit like it was cute or something.

Without thinking, I reached over and yanked her by her coat. We tussled for a minute, and then she got the best of me and caused my lip split. I snatched my gun from under my skirt out it's holster and popped two in the bitch. She held her chest in shock, but since this was a lil pap pap, you could barely hear the shots go off. I stood up, dusted myself off, and watched her die slowly.

"Bet you next time. Oh, wait, there won't be a next time, bitch!"

I□ laughed all the way to my car feeling good. Wait 'til I□ tell Quell this shit. He thought he had the perfect girl, but all she did was help plan him a trip to three hots and a cot.

Chapter 35

Akeem

I watched my phone ring a few times from Shidah calling me. She was relentless too. If I didn't already think she was suspect, then that alone would have turned me off. I had to fall back from her just a lil bit to clear my head and really think about who the hell was she. I couldn't help but conclude that she had to be one of the babes setting people up. Them bitches had just vanished since I got word on them.

Now, all of a sudden, she pops up, and then the bitch that Hasan fucks with. The only thing that's pissing me off more is, I can't seem to find any information on any of them. It appears they are just regular women, but I can probably prove some shit if I find out they are related. Shit, if I can figure out if they sisters, cousins, or something, then I'd be on to something. For right now, I guess the only way I'm a find out is if I stay fucking with this broad.

I didn't like the sound of that, but at this point, if I wanted to stay ahead of the game, then I better take this one for the team. Shiid, Has too. I was glad I did tell him to just watch the bitch a lil closer. Knowing his loosely screwed ass, he was probably gon' have her feeling weird as hell. They'd fuck around and shoot each other out of fear of what the other can do.

I had just picked up money from a loyal customer who always borrows and always has my shit on time. I just wished that they all could be like that and I didn't have to kill anybody, but it never works out that way.

Shidah was calling me again, and I sighed as I pulled the phone up to my ear to answer.

"What's up"

"I would like to know what I did for you to be straight up watching me call you."

I looked around just to make sure the bitch wasn't watching me.

"You a fraud, lil momma. I don't deal with those kind."

"A fraud? What are you talking about, Akeem?"

"Look, I ain't about to sit up here and go into details about something you know about already."

"Well, can you make some time today for us to talk? You can come by here maybe around six?"

I looked at the phone, and that was three hours from now. I really didn't want to do it, but fuck it. Let's see what she gon' say about an empty apartment that she says she had for a while.

I went home, washed my sack, and just threw on a Champion sweat suit with my Timbs. It was one of those kind of days. I ain't feel like all the extra shit, but I made sure my gun was loaded, and with an extra clip. This time, when I got there, I immediately noticed a difference. She had decorated the place nicely. I wasn't sure if I wanted to sit down or not, but she was on me.

"Damn, Akeem, can you at least come and sit ya ass down? I don't bite… I mean, unless you want me to," she flirted.

I smirked and took a seat. She started pulling out snacks and my favorite wine again. This chick really thinks she got me wrapped.

"So, what did I do for you to say I'm a fraud?" she asked, getting right down to it.

"How long you been here?"

"I told you, a couple months. And the only reason why it was so empty last time is because I had just officially moved in. I got the place but still stayed with my mom for a few. Now, I'm here. Is that why you said that?"

I ain't answer her because I still didn't believe that shit. But I let it go, for now. She entertained me for a few more hours. Even sucking the soul of my body then giving it back with her pussy. She had some fire to her, I will give her that, but she isn't to be trusted.

Chapter 36

Travis

"Baby, did I do something wrong?"
My face balled up at her asking me that.
"What? No. Why you talking like that?"
"Because you seem to be changing on me."
I got up from where I was sitting and went to cradle
her. If she said I was changing, then I had to be doing
too much talking to Camille. I ain't think I switched up
my patterns at all, but somehow Emana had noticed,
and I can't have baby girl feeling like that.
"Naw baby, you ain't do shit, and if you feel I'm
changing, then I'm sorry. I hadn't noticed myself."
She looked me in my eyes to see if I was lying. I
couldn't tell if she saw the truth or not, but I stood my
ground. I had plans to link up with Camille later that
day, but I cancelled them by just not going. I stayed in
the house with my girl for the rest of the night, giving
her the attention she needed.
My phone even went on DND, just so she couldn't call
or text. It wasn't like I was being mean or saying fuck
her, I just didn't want the mix up. On my way to work
the next morning, the moment I turned my shit on
regular, she was calling. I waited until my lunch break
to answer. She went off on me, saying I was treating
her like a clown and a whole bunch of other shit. At
that moment, I realized she was in deeper than what
we were supposed to be.

Truthfully, we may not have been on no couple type time, but we did put in a lot of it. Emana pointing out that I'm different, is all I need to get my shit together. I liked Camille, she was crazy straight, but I loved Mana. She had my heart. In a perfect world, having them both would be cool. Now, I just have to break it down to her somehow without the drama.

She asked a million questions about me standing her up yesterday, and since I ain't feel the need to answer her, I just said I got tied up. That was the worst answer I could have given because I started to see a side I never knew she had. She made my decision to leave her alone that much easier from the shit that was coming out of her mouth. I always try to be the chill one, more level headed, but I could easily kill this bitch.

How the hell we go from chilling and enjoying each other's company to her coming at my neck all crazy and saying I'm a bitch nigga. She acted like she ain't know from off top that I have a girl. I just hung up, and this time blocked her. I ain't got to deal with that shit from her or any other bitch when mine don't even talk like that. Who the fuck raised her dumb ass?

Chapter 37

Hasan

I knew I wasn't tripping when I saw the same car twice. And it just so happened that today I was sitting off in the cut watching the streets. But, I was glad I was because the streets were also watching me. The black Monte Carlo circled the block more than once riding slow on my jinther. Y'all already know I only use the car to do dirty shit in, so who the fuck was checking my shit out? I didn't budge from where I was. I was hoping that whoever it was would get out and show their face.

That never happened. After the last time, they just pulled off. I still sat for a minute, waiting to see if anything else was moving. But everything kind of died down, and got quiet for the most part. I walked out from the cut and hit the corner. A car started speeding real fast, and with no questions asked, I whopped down on that bitch, causing it to hit another parked car at the end of the street.

I wanted to see if it was somebody that I knew, so I ran up on it guns drawn ready for some more wreck. The driver head was splattered all across the dash board. His shit was so mangled I couldn't recognized him. But any minute people were going to start forming crowds out here and I didn't feel like having to kill somebody else just to cover this shit up.

Sprinting off to the crib, I go the fuck out of there. I wanted to believe that, the speeding car and the other one circling the block was all for me. If so, I just got to watch out and have an extra clip on me. I was just about to chill out for the night until Nia texted me talking that I miss you shit. And I was in the mood to buss down her walls so I got shitty fresh and hopped in my wheel to the bachelor pad.

She really thought this was my spot. And found herself leaving lil shit here to put her mark on it. I ain't care cause lately I haven't really brought nobody else here. If I did slide up in something I was at their crib and out by the time their man got home. Yeah, these bitches ain't loyal and been for everybody. I had about two that I fuck whenever they called because it was trouble in paradise.

Wasn't my problem they preferred this Mandingo over that. She wasn't too far behind me when I got there. When she walked up, her smile was bright like she was really happy to see a nigga. I shook my head and pulled her inside.

"Why you shaking ya head ugly?" Nia wrapped her arms around me getting on her toes for a kiss.

This girl loved putting her lips on me. You already know that kiss turned into some steamy wet ass sex. Ever since I dropped this shit off in her draws, lil momma couldn't get enough. My only hope is that she wasn't one of them bitches. That shit would have me fucked up cause she growing on a nigga and I would definitely have to kill her ass. All Nia wanted to do was cuddle now. She be all under me where as I can barely move around. I don't know whether to like it or despise it.

Before we could even finish blowing one she was knocked out on my lap. Like any other time, I picked her up and carried her to the bed. While she was sleeping peacefully I went and grabbed her phone. I just wanted to see if she had anything in there that would send them Suwu flags up. Her phone was locked, but it had the finger print code on it. I quietly and carefully picked up her thumb to open it.

I must have really gang walked in that pussy for her to be that knocked out. Sitting back down in the living room, I smoked on my bud and scrolled through her phone from every message to the call log. I didn't see anything that would stand out, so I put her shit back where it was, double locked the crib up, and got in bed with her.

I'm not gon say she off the hook, but she can be my boo thang until a nigga know something.

Chapter 38

Rashidah

After that last encounter with Akeem and him leaving me like that, then not having any words for me, I knew it had something to do with the crib. I took my time going out for three days straight, finding stuff to make it look like a real home that a girl like myself lives at. I knew I did the damn thing because although his face never switched up, I can still tell he was surprised to see it looked different in there.

I mean he didn't even want to sit next to me, when all I kept thinking about was what he carried around in his pants. A few times I woke up sweating, because in my dream, he was doggie this pussy. But that was the problem, it was just a dream. I cursed myself for falling for this nigga. I was on a mission to get him for his paper but yet, now my mission is solely intended to capture his heart and have him looking at me through different eyes.

I'm far from a dumb bitch and I know he doesn't really fuck with me like that. I see the faces he does make when I'm over stepping my boundaries. I get it, I just can't help myself to be after him though. It's all his fault. He put up that chase like I wasn't shit and that just made me go harder. But fa' real, I wasn't expecting my damn engine to go in that new car I got. It was fate that it just so happened to be him that came to my rescue.

The moment he loosened up a lil, I hopped right on his ass letting him serve me up a dose of 'Best Dick'. That's exactly what it is. Specially anytime he got me, Rashidah, out of character. I wasn't even acting like this with my ex in the beginning. Before he started showing me his true colors. Only if my sisters knew how I was really getting down, they probably would never look up to me again. All the rules have been broken.

I played a big part in being strong and saying fuck these niggas, just so they could have the same attitude and energy about it. And I know I was wrong for leading them on to being this way, especially with me not practicing what I preach, but shit. Stuff happens. Akeem happened. And with that being said, I walked into the crib I shared with my sisters about to break the news to them that I was moving out.

I figured if I was gon be paying for a crib that I decked out, why not just move in that bitch.

"Where you been?" Camille asked with an attitude like I was her child.

I laughed right in her face and took a seat. These last few days she had gone from happy to mad black woman, well mixed women. Nia had just come down the steps with her phone glued to her ear smiling at the same time feeding her face. I motioned to her that I need to talk, and she held up her finger.

Nia joined the rest of us as everybody's eyes were trained on me, and Camille was stilling sitting there with her face balled up. Well, if that shit was balled now, wait until they hear this.

"So, y'all, I just wanted to tell you guys that I am moving out?"

"What?"

"Wait, why?"

"Yeah, what the fuck is really going on for you to just want to up and leave us all of a sudden?" Camille interrogated nastily, making us all look at her like she had five heads.

If she kept it up, we were going to be going toe to toe. I rolled my eyes at her then resumed my conversation.

"I know this is short notice, but I have a place that I been keeping a secret. And before you guys jump on my case, it was for reasonable cause. I just decided that now, I'm going to go head and move in. This crib is all paid for, y'all just really have to pay the utilities here." Now all their necks were popping and eyes were rolling.

"Okay, so what about this whole setting the brothers up?" Simone scooted up to the edge of her seat and waited to see what I was gon' say about that.

"As for now, just fall back, and once I get settled and see where this shit is all going, then I will let y'all know how to move from there."

They gave me that 'I don't believe you' look, and I thought I saw Nia exhale along with Simone. I was done with this conversation, so I got up and went to my room to look at the stuff that I wanted to take and separate it from the things that will stay there just in case.

Chapter 39

Jequell

Hearing the news I heard, I wasn't sure if I wanted to be happy or fucked up about it. My lawyer told me some girl by the name of Shyanne helped the rollers find where my location was. I thought that was a low blow for her, and I vowed to put my hands so tight around her neck until the bitch popped. But I ain't have to. The next day, I got more news that she was killed outside her crib.

I was hoping that my brothers got wind of that shit and were the ones who took care of her, but they said they found out too late, and that somebody else did her in. That shit was weird. Was she doing some shit behind my back that I had no clue of and it caught up to her? the whole situation had me having mixed emotions and shit. Bittersweet.

On a brighter note, I was getting patted down to go out on a visit. I hadn't had one of these since the last time Simone fell through, and I hadn't really talked to her like that. It's all good though, no hard or ill feeling toward her. She just came into my life, so I wasn't really expecting her to be on this bus ride with me. But I was curious to know who was here to see a nigga. I had told my bros they don't have to come up here anymore.

I knew how they all felt about being behind these walls even if it was for a visit. Once the guard gay ass finished shaking my nuts, I went out, and at the table sat Simone, looking all good. Next to her was my momma. I had to double take like 'what the fuck was this?' My ma got up breaking her face smiling and hugged me so tight. Then Simone did the same but planted some wet kisses on my lips. She grabbed my dick too before sitting back down.

Now I'm at the table with a rock-hard penis wanting to lay her ass across it spread eagle and beat her shit into it. The way we were seated, she was close enough to me that I slid my hand up her dress and found bare pussy. I couldn't resist sticking my fingers in there. She was so moist, I had to make sure one of us was talking at all times because she started to moan a lil and her shit was gushing.

I felt like my shit was going to pop out of my blues any minute if I kept it up. But it was no turning back now. She was at the edge of her seat rocking back and forth on my hand. My ma got up and excused herself to the bathroom. I think she knew what we were doing. Once her nectar trickled down my fingers, I took them out from under the table and sucked them clean. Her pussy was so fresh and smelled like water but with a hint of roses.

"What you doing here and with my leading lady?"

"I had to come see you, and ya momma and I have been real close lately. I hope that doesn't bother you."

"It will if you tryna get something out of it. But if you really around 'cause you fuck with a nigga then naw, I don't mind, but my brothers will"

"Yeah, I know. One of them walked in when I was there, and he did not like the idea of me sitting at ya momma house," she told me with disdain on her face. I told her to watch herself, those were my brothers she was talking about.

"And what you mean if I'm trying to get something out of it? What is there to get, Jequell? Look where you are," she said waving her hand around the V.I.

She had a point but you still never know with these females now and days. When my momma came back, she asked did we get our freak shit all out, cause she can step off again. I flashed a big smile while Simone looked away red and embarrassed. The way they interacted with one and other had me perplexed like a mafucka. They sure were pretty tight. I made a mental note to hit up Akeem and Hasan.

I know she said he was there and wasn't too happy about her being there. I knew my brothers and any new face will have them looking sideways at cha'. For now, I will put the word in that she can get a pass, but any goofy shit, she can get checked also. Riding for me or not. I ain't got no picks.

Chapter 40

Nia

I couldn't move this morning, I was just feeling very tired. My legs were heavy and wobbly like jello. I wasn't sure what the issue is, but I thought maybe if I take another nap, and once I get up, I will be good. All my sisters were gone, and I called my ma' to see if she could come over. She said let her finish up her food and she will be right over. I laid back down and pulled the covers up.

And the moment I drifted off into a god sleep my loud ass ringer woke me up. I was soooo irritated that I automatically started cussing in a different language from English the second I picked up the phone.

"Aye, Nia, you better calm that bullshit down, girl. I don't know what the fuck you saying, and don't care to know." Soon as I heard his voice, I switched back to my regular self.

"Hey boo, I'm sorry. I don't feel so good this morning and all I want to do is sleep. It was just getting good when you called setting me off."

"Damn, well what's wrong? Something hurt on ya body?"

"I really don't know, I just feel different." I whined.

He offered to come get me to take me to his crib to lounge for the day. I thought long and hard about that, not sure if it was such a good idea for him to come here, but I don't want to be alone. Even though my ma said she was coming, I kind of wanted to be with him. Hmmm, decisions.

Saying fuck it, I sent him the address playing it off as if it was my cousin crib. He said he didn't give a damn if it was my nigga crib, he was on his way. That made me smile and think that he somewhat cared about me. With the lil bit of strength I had, I swung my legs over and grabbed a hoodie to throw over my night gown. Yeah, it was this type of party. I wasn't putting any effort into getting dressed. Today he will see me for who I really am.

I have slowly been coming around to being myself around him, and I must say I think it's the same way with him too. Well, at least I think it is. I heard a horn beeping, I wish he could just come in here and carry me out, but that's doing too much. I can walk it just feels weird. Sending him a text that I was coming. Guess I was taking too long because by the time I got down to the end of the steps he was out the car and banging on the door.

I laughed as I slowly walked over it.

"Really, Hasan? I told you I was coming."

"Yeah, you were taking too long, had to make sure you were good in here," he said, sticking his head in the door and looking around.

"Aww, you care, baby?" I teased.

"Shut ya ass up."

I had him carry my bag out and he bitched about that. As I walked down the steps to the car I almost forgot about my ma' was supposed to come over. I hit the call log calling her back.

"Yes chica, you okay? You want me to come now?"

"No, Ma, I was calling to tell you never mind."

"Uh, okay. You sure baby?"

"Yes, ma'am, I'm good. I'm just going to go back to sleep."

She was reluctant to hang up thinking that something was really wrong, but I didn't care to get into telling her that I was with my boo. Someone who I set out, to set up, but ended up getting my heart caught up, so now I want a real relationship with him.

As we rode the streets, I wondered what he thought of me. Like how did he feel and will this possible go anywhere? I felt like if I asked, it would have him viewing me differently. And everything right now was going pretty good, I kind of don't want to fuck with that. Soon as he parked and I opened the door, a wave of nausea came over me, causing me to sit back and chill for a second.

"Nia what you doing? Come on." I put a finger up telling him to give me a minute. He rounded the car and stood in front of me, just observing me closely.

"Yo, you really don't look so good. Want me to take you to the hospital?"

I looked up at him first, not really wanting to deal with emergency rooms and whatnot, but I never felt like this before, and for the first time I was scared. I shook my head yes, and he got back in the car to take me there.

Chapter 41

Travis

Emana usually leaves for work before me sometimes, and this morning, like any other, she did. But soon as she closed the front door, she opened it right back up, screaming my name at the top of her lungs. Shit scared the fuck out of me. I grabbed my gun from under my pillow and hopped up with just my briefs on, running to where she was. Her face was so mad, for a second, I thought I did something.

Slowly, I approached her, and her eyes went from me to my gun then back up to me.

"Baby, what's wrong? Why you hollering?"

She didn't say anything, she just left back out the door, and I followed her.

"What the fuck!!"

Somebody had flattened all her tires and three of mine. Shit, they might as well had gone on ahead and did the forth one too. Fucking clowns!

"Who would do something like this? I don't bother anybody?" Mana began crying.

I rocked her, saying it was going to be alright and we would get the tires fixed today. I called up Hasan, and he said he was tied up at the moment. I knew Akeem was probably at work, so I had no choice but to call my pop.

Mana was an hour late to work, but she thanked my dad a million times for taking her. She didn't have much to say to me, and I felt some type about that. She acted like I did it. Pissed, I called into work and told them what happened. My boss was cool and took me off the schedule for the day. My pop took me to a few spots to get used tires for my car, but I went to Pep Boys and got brand new tires for her wheel.

"Son, you cheating on that girl?"

That question threw me off, but I wasn't, though.

"No, Pop, why you ask me that?"

"'Cause this has a women written all over it. And if you not cheating on her then you have bigger problems then you think." I

sat back and thought about what he said. Then it hit me that only other person that could have done this was Camille's nerd ass, on the hood. Our last conversation was a lil while ago, and I thought she just took heed to what I said and got the fuck on. But somehow, she found out where we stay and decided to fuck with, not only my car, but hers too.

Soon as my pop and I changed all the tires on both cars, he drove behind me in mine to her job where I dropped her car off to her. She thanked me but still was pissed. I mean, she had every right to be, and if it really was Camille, then I can see how she probably thinks I'm cheating. Specially if my old man said it. Fuck!

These are problems I swear I don't want to have crim. I ain't even fuck the dizzy bitch and she already acting like a bitter ex. I held small talk on the way back to the house, but my mind was somewhere else. I really didn't know the first place to look for this broad, that left me no choice but to call her.

"What, Travis?" she answered all impolite like I was bothering her.

"Yo, Camille, you on some nut shit, I see."

"I'm sorry, nut shit? I beg to differ."

She was making me furious as shit with the way she was playing this whole thing off. And by talking to her, there was no doubt in my mind that she definitely did the shit. Seemed like the only way to get her back was to play nice. But what I had in store for her was way worse then she could have expected from a nigga like me. There ain't a soul out here that will fuck with my family! And I can already see if I don't take care of this shit, it will later become a problem.

Chapter 42

Hasan

The nut ass doctors ran so many tests on lil momma that I was getting antsy as shit just sitting there and watching it happen. When I first picked her up, I wanted to be nosey and see if I could connect some type of dots, leaving me to never really pay her close attention. When I did, her face was pale as shit, and she really didn't look so good. Now, my black ass was in the hospital with her and wishing I at least had something to smoke on me, but I didn't.

When she sent me the address, I hopped right up, leaving everything but my gun. I ain't forget about that shit that happened the other day. And whoever it was better come a lil harder than that. I'm a fucking vet at this shit! I wondered what Trav could have wanted, I was so busy listening to everything that was being said between Nia and the nurses that I told him I was tied up.

But while I was just sitting here waiting, I texted him to see if he was good. He said he had to tell me something, but it can wait until later. I chilled, I knew we were going to be here for a minute. Guess that's what I get for being all nice trying do shit a nigga had no business doing. But I wasn't a frauding ass nigga ,and I can't front, I actually like lil momma, for what it's worth.

They put her on something, so right now she just sleeping. I couldn't help but take my phone out and snap a few pics of her. Nia was beautiful, and ain't no denying that. She was growing on me so much that I was developing something small for her. I just hope ain't no crafty shit jumping off. After a small knock caused her to wake up, the doctor walked in all chipper. He had enough energy for three people.

"So, Ms. Henderson, after running a few tests and finding nothing, the issue to this lil problem is, you are pregnant, honey."

We both sat up at the same time. The room started spinning, and I had to hold my head. I can't even count how many times we done went raw. Fuck!! This was a major fuck up on my part for not strapping up. A few times, she seduced me, and putting one on was the furthest thing from my mind.

She finished talking to the doc, and I was about ready to go at that point. They told her they will be back with her discharge papers.

"Aye, I'm a go get the wheel. You can come out by yaself, right?"

She rolled her sad eyes and shook her head yes.

The whole walk to the car I thought about what I wanted to do about this situation. I wasn't a slob ass nigga, and if she wasn't fucking on nothing else, then I'll take care of mine. I mean, that's if she wants to keep it.

I pulled up in the front and waited a good 10 minutes until she appeared walking the same as before if not slower. Reaching across, I opened the door for her as she eased in.

"We still going to the spot?"

With a head nod, she turned her back and leaned against the door. Nia was already not saying much the first time, but she was completely mute now. I ain't know how to take her because this just wasn't her attitude. She was a feisty ass woman, and that was what I liked the most about her.

We got to the spot, and this time I helped her out the car. I had been there so much that I had moved some of my personal stuff here. I still didn't tell her about my real crib, and I also still believe she doesn't need to know at this point.

Nia kicked her shoes off and pulled her hoodie off, going straight to the bed. That was cool for me. I rolled up so fast, I almost got a fucking headache. But after I was good and high, I went to the kitchen and found us something to eat. I wasn't a chef, but I knew how to do something if my ass was hungry.

Since I had some chipped steak, I cut it up and made us some cheese steaks with fries. Sprinkling Old Bay over them with salt. She wasn't asleep when I entered the room, but she was just lying there with tears falling down her face.

"Nia, why you crying, ma? Is it because of what the doctor said?"

She focused in on me and said yeah, barely above a whisper.

"Listen, if you don't want to keep the baby then don't. Either way I'll be around." I got up to leave, but she grabbed my arm and pulled me back.

"The issue is not the baby, well it is. But I want to keep it. I want to keep you. I also feel that, even though, you saying you gon' be here with what eva decision I make, if I go get an abortion, you gon' cut me off. I don't want that." She really looked paranoid about this shit.

"Keep it then, Nia. What is so hard about that?"

"Only if you knew," she responded, wiping her face then sitting up to eat.

I wasn't gon' play a fucking guessing game with her about shit. If she ain't want to tell me the real reason why she can't keep the baby, then I don't need to fucking know. And yeah, she right. I wasn't expecting the answer to her problem to be a baby, but I damn sure don't mind being a father either.

Chapter 43

Camille

I thought that nigga would see it my way. Sooner rather than later he was going to be calling me. I had my resources, and I found out where he lived with his precious bitch. He had the right fucking one talking that shit to me on the phone. I just wanted to know why he stood me up. Plus, I called him way too many times for my own liking, and I got no answer until the next day. His ass was being all nonchalant like we weren't supposed to go somewhere, and that pissed me all the way off.

Late night, I crept over there with my handy blade and slashed all her tires but left one of his untouched. That was just to be smart. When the morning hit, I was up running around already, but I knew the second my phone vibrated it was him. Now he talking about seeing me. I started to say no, but figured I have a few more tricks up my sleeve.

And now that I know just how much he loves his bitch, I was gon' blackmail his ass. He was supposed to be meeting me at this place, but he just texted and said he had to do something and was gon' be a few hours. He said he will call me soon as he was done. I got annoyed, but what the hell. I finished up my errands and went on home. When I left, Nia was still there and looked like she wasn't going anywhere any time soon, but her room was empty.

I shrugged it off and warmed up a Jamaican beef patty that Simone made. I just needed something to take my anti-depressant pills. Yes, sometimes I do feel like I'm depressed, and these pills help me feel normal. Only my ma knows about them because she went with me to the doctor that day. After I finished eating and cleaned up my lil mess, the urge to take a nap came through strong.

My room was too far right now, so I curled up on the couch and made sure my phone was on a high ringer so when he did call, I would hear it. Don't know how long I was out, but I woke up to slobber dripping down the side of my mouth on the pillow. Gathering myself, I wiped it and got up to go take care of the pillow.

I tripped when I noticed that Travis was sitting in the chair watching the whole time. I couldn't read his demeanor, and at this point, that didn't even matter.

I never told him where I lived, and for him to be there, in our home wasn't good. I smelled danger. Quickly, I tried to run to the kitchen where I left my purse. It held my gun, but that failed, especially when he stuck his foot out making me fall completely. That didn't stop me, though. I was determined to kill this nigga before he killed me. When he saw me crawling, he got up and dragged me back to the living room.

"Where do you think you going, baby? I thought you wanted to see a nigga, but now you running. Hmm, I don't get it," he toyed with me.

I actually felt kind of scared of this nigga. He never gave me the impression that he was crazy, but I should have known better. He took the gun he was holding and dragged it from my face, around my cheek bones, down to my pelvic area. He demanded that I come out of my clothes, leaving me with nothing on but my bra.

Travis used his gun to fuck me, causing my shit to split and coat the tip of the gun red. This was pure fun to him because he kept a smile on his face when all I wanted was for one of my sisters to walk in and splat this nigga for violating me. He pinched my nipple so hard, I screamed. And that made him smack the fuck out of me.

"See, I was willing to let us be, but no, you had to go above and beyond fucking with shit that was no business of yours. I love my girl to death, and I can't have a shiesty bitch like yaself walking around when I know you can cause her or me harm. Now with that being said, Camille, you got to go, baby girl."

He pulled out the same blade I used to flatten their tires and dangled it in front of my face.

"Looks familiar, don't it?"

I backed up into the couch not saying anything.

I knew what that knife could do. Too many times I saw the life leave somebody's body by that very thing there. He plunged it right into my heart. I wanted to protest and fight, but I couldn't. Travis turned it and jiggled it then pulled it out. I fell over and thought about all the bodies we caught, my old life and my new one, my sisters, then my ma. I just hoped that they would find out that he was the one who took me out, and kill him and that bitch!

To be continued...

CPSIA information can be obtained
at www.ICGtesting.com
Printed in the USA
LVHW08s2105280818
588394LV00011B/1085/P